Madame O

Robert Montagnese

Cover photography & design by Andy Johanson

ISBN 9781793978417

This is a work of fiction. Names, characters, businesses, places, events, locales, and incidents are either the products of the author's imagination or used in a fictitious manner. Any resemblance to actual persons, living or dead, or actual events is purely coincidental.

For John, Maryanne, and Andy, without them this would never be.

Authors Note

Over the many years visiting St. John U.S. Virgin Island, I have searched to find coral that has washed up on the shore. I remember my first in the shape of something familiar, a statue rather unique in the world. The coral shape to my eye was that of the Winged Victory.

The treasured Winged Victory resides in Paris at the Louvre having traveled many centuries ago from Greece. Her history is fascinating. Always true to her purpose she was a beacon to guide sailors safely back from defending what they believed was good.

Many of us have seen a photo of her or perhaps remember her in the movie *Funny Face,* as she stands behind Audrey Hepburn who swiftly descends the staircase that leads up to the statue. In her current residence, she continues to inspire.

For whatever we lose

(like a you or a me).

It's always our self we find

in the sea.

\- E. E. Cummings

Chapter One

"International World Journal"

Returning home from a European business trip I was comfortably seated in a first-class seat on the aisle, of course. Shortly after take-off I opened the complimentary *International World Journal* newspaper. In the business section of the paper I came across an article I found interesting *Twenty-Five Years Ago, Today*. As I finished reading it a perky flight attendant delivered my vodka martini, one olive only. Moments later she returned with a small bowl of warm nuts apparently fresh out of the galley microwave. I took a long sip of my drink setting the nuts aside and neatly tore the article out of the paper. I placed it into my Mulberry address book and shifted my attention to my drink ultimately giving in to eating the nuts.

Twenty-Five Years Ago, Today

Twenty-five years ago, at the bicentennial celebration of Columbia University, Dr. J. Robert Oppenheimer, spoke on the topic of the isolation of the artist and scientist. Dr. Oppenheimer was the former director of the Atomic Laboratories in New Mexico where the atomic bomb had been perfected. His speech was the last in a year-long bicentennial celebration at the university. In his speech, Oppenheimer made no reference to his recent dismissal from the Commission on Atomic Energy denying him further access to all classified data. Oppenheimer's message in the closing speech at Columbia may be both a circuitous apology as well as a warning to his community of scholars. "Physicists are interested in new things, constantly seeking discoveries that can change our world for the advancement of mankind. However, sometimes political motives may compromise the creator's original intent and the results become catastrophic." It was a somber ending for the bicentennial celebration.

Chapter Two

"Sea Grapes"

It was always during the month of March, it marked the annual celebration of John's birthday, the 12th to be exact, the same day the Girl Scouts was founded. A fact that he never forgets to mention when asked about his special day (still makes me smile every time). We would travel and vacation on St. John U.S. Virgin Islands and always stay at Kokomo Cottage. The cottage that we rented is centered on Bordeaux Mountain with a spectacular view of the British Virgin Islands. In fact, *Caribbean Life and Travel* reported that the vistas from this location offered some of the best views of the Caribbean. John and I fell in love with the place the first time we saw it. Over time things have changed on the island, some islanders say not for the better, but at Kokomo time is considerate, nothing changes except that which the sea air chooses to embrace.

It is a rather treacherous driveway leading to the cottage. In four-wheel drive one travels at almost a 90-degree angle down a dirt road that provides little margin for error. One slip and you could become a memory among the wild goats who graze below. With cautious maneuvering, you arrive at the makeshift car park made from coral and broken shells. It's only after you've set the emergency brake one can take a breath. The storybook white picket fence that purple begonias creep around, is a welcoming entrance to the cottage. Entering Kokomo, you can't help but to grin looking at the palette of pastel colors and a view of the shimmering blue-green sea off in the distance. Inside is a large 4 post mahogany bed, a table and two chairs and a wicker loveseat. The furnishings are simple, neat and comfortable. The delightful discovery, even after all these years, is the outside veranda facing Coral Bay. When we are not on the beach this is where we spend our time watching the ships in the distance bob and sway in the water below.

We can see Virgin Gorda from the veranda of the Cottage. The island is named for its shape. The peak to the south end is rounded and as it declines creates a silhouette resembling sumptuous breasts. Toward the west, shapely curves in the terrain suggest that of her ample thighs and the slender lines of her legs. Where the mountain meets the sea, cliffs emerge to reveal two graceful feet. In her repose, she is continuously bathed by the turbulent surf that surrounds her. At night her crown, a waterfall of stars overhead, appears while she rests peacefully in state.

On our first day, we got up early to travel to the windward side of the island to explore the beach and take in sun. As in the past we challenged ourselves to find a remote location and this time we worked our way along a jungle path along Leinster Bay. We read long ago that the Bay was quite an important location for trading during the island's Dutch occupation. Along the shoreline there was a pack of wild donkeys roaming and up on a hill the skeletal remains of an abandoned sugar mill. In the past, we would pass by the place in search of a spot on the beach but this time we decided to explore it. The Park's Service plaque at the footpath's entrance to the plantation indicated it was the Annaberg Plantation. John removed the guidebook from his bag and read about its history and we quickly discovered we were standing on ground that were once slave quarters. Out of respect we walked in silence witnessing what remained of the decaying stone structures. Painful behavior of the past permeated the earth below. In our path were uneasy shadows, a quiet stillness in the air.

A stretch of beach where crystal blue water rides the white sand in a lazy soft rhythm is where we choose to spend our day.

We took in the sweet sea breeze and were thankful for our good fortune. We lingered for hours and found some shade under a tree to have our lunch. After a last swim and the mandatory first day sunburn, we loaded our Jeep and headed into town to pick up supplies for sunset cocktails. Having secured the provisions for the evening we headed back to the Cottage. Just as we approached, a very large boulder appeared on the side of the road, known on the island as Easter Rock. John slowed down to take the sharp curve. It was at that moment we noticed something hidden among the trees.

John pulled off the road and so close to the side of the mountain that I needed to slide across the front seat maneuvering over the gearshift to get out of the Jeep! Once out of the vehicle, I followed him down the path to inspect our discovery. It was an iron gate. We walked down an abandoned path to examine it. Intrigued by its ornate design and discrete location I asked John what he thought was beyond it. There was a thick cover of vines on both sides of the gate making it difficult to get to the other side. The gate was secured with a rusty lock and chain wrapped twice around for added protection. Although the lock was rusted with age it remained strong enough to keep us out. Stepping back, we noticed fragmented letters that spanned across the arched structure on top. What did remain intact on top of the gate were the letters O P E I E R.

As sunset approached we headed home aware that the bag of ice for our drinks was beginning to melt, making a chilled martini difficult to achieve later. The evening plans were for us to meet our friend Judy, who owns Kokomo, at Miss Lucy's, a beach restaurant, for dinner.

Judy has been living full time on the island for over 25 years and always reminds us that she never goes out at night except when we are there. The restaurant is a favorite of ours. It is a very casual flip-flop joint which is why we like it. The entrance in the front yard is always reserved for Miss Lucy's goats, so one walks around to the back of the place where plastic tables and chairs are randomly placed on an uneven concrete patio that slopes down to the water on the shore. Upon arrival, we were seated below an enormous Sea Grape tree with limbs almost as large as its trunk. On past visits the waxy green foliage provided coverage from the light tropical rain that is typical this time of year. Admiring the stretched limbs of the tree John mentioned our trek into the old sugar mill when our waitress arrived with menus.

"Yes, we had never walked up the hill to check out the old place. I was glad that I had my guidebook on me to learn about it, how tragic and all." John took a sip of his drink and I jumped into the conversation.

"Have you ever been up there?" I asked Judy.

"There seems to be a weird, no, not weird, a dark, yes, that is the word I meant to say, a dark energy about the place. I've never seen slave quarters until today. It's so sad." I then looked over the menu. Our waitress returned as John was asking Judy if she knew anything about the iron-gate down the road from Easter Rock.

"We were driving back from Mongoose Junction when we saw this iron gate set back from the road. Had I not looked out at the water below I would have missed it." Judy said she never explored the site and didn't know much about it. While a second round of drinks was being served, John tried to describe the exact location of the gate.

"You know that sharp turn just as you start to head up toward the only intersection on that side of the mountain?" As he was describing the location I noticed that our waitress seemed to take an interest that went beyond our appetites. Her inquisitive behavior caught my attention.

No more than 11, she lingered by our table even after she delivered our drinks as if to learn more about our discovery that day. She was a beautiful young girl. Her skin was the color of milk chocolate and smooth as porcelain. In the candle light her eyes sparkled a green like that of an early spring grass. We had never seen her during our past visits and were told by Judy it was because she had been living on St. Thomas with her cousin for most of her childhood. Her trance-like state was broken by the sudden appearance of an older black woman.

"Isabel!" The woman shouted. "What in God's mercy are you doing girl? Move on with your duties." It startled us for a minute, then the old woman went on. "Child mind your own business or the devil himself will be tempted to lend you a hand minding his."

It was Miss Lucy herself. The old woman smiled politely and walked away. She was on the other side of middle age with the marks of a hard life etched into her face.

Chapter Three

"The Iron Gate"

Having learned very little about the gate from Judy the night before we decided to return and explore it for ourselves the next day. Our plan was to go beyond the gate and see what was below. Surely there was something of interest down on the beach, otherwise, why the gate? After our breakfast, we loaded the Jeep with supplies for the day. The cooler we packed contained tuna salad sandwiches, chips, bottled water and two bottles of a lovely Pinot Grigio packed in ice.

Arriving at the destination we parked on the side of the road as we did the day before. We knew the chain with the double lock would keep us from entering through the gate so we worked our way around the side of it, clearing vines out of the way, making just enough room for us to pass around with our supplies in hand. Once inside, we headed down the path, occasionally looking back to see if anyone was watching. Towards the bottom the path widened to what became an abandoned road that trailed off into a jungle like terrain. When we got to the bottom we expected to find something more than the road but all we saw was a white sandy beach. We lingered on the beach for a while, having lunch and talking about the end of our iron gate adventure. After our lunch John suggested we go for a swim. Wading into the water up to our knees until we took the plunge, immediately the chilly water cleared our heads from too many "refreshments" the night before.

Swimming out further into the crystal blue water we didn't think there was anything out of the ordinary and wondered why there was even a gate up by the road. We laughed about discovering this perfect private beach as we drifted further out in the water. It was then that we noticed a hidden structure just off the beach.

As we swam towards shore the structure became more visible through the island greenery that shielded it. We reached the beach in a matter of minutes and found a pathway leading to what appeared to be an abandoned home. As we got closer, we realize that it was a 2-story structure. The windows were all boarded except for two on the second floor. Walking around to the back there was a stone chimney that felt warm to the touch. I thought it seemed odd but John said that maybe it was from the sun.

Next to the chimney, the remains of a concrete patio with seashells inlaid in an artistically created star burst pattern lead to a back door. All at once we both noticed a figure off in the distance among the vegetation. It was then we sensed we were being watched.

Without saying a word John and I quickly made it to our towels and headed to the path leading to the road. When we reached the top, we made another discovery, the iron gate was unlocked.

"Who was that?" John asked as he started the Jeep.

"Haven't a clue but let's get the heck out of here quick," I said while I was buckling my seat belt.

"You think we are in trouble?" He said to me as he pulled onto the road.

"For what, trespassing?" I replied.

John then looked over and said. "No, not that. I can't put my finger on what is bothering me about this, but there's something about the gate and that house."

We headed back to our cottage. John stepped on the gas. Once we gained some distance he spoke again.

"Obviously, whomever it was watching us had keys to the locked gate."

"You are making me nervous." I replied anxiously.

"Really Mister, whose idea was it to go back there this morning?" He said back to me. He was right. It was my idea I thought to myself as we drove in silence.

It didn't take too long to get back to the cottage thanks to John's lead foot. When we backed down the driveway we discovered a note tacked to the white picket fence. We expected it would be from Judy.

Sirs,

I am not often inclined to provide advice to visitors here on St. John, but I believe it is something that I must do to protect things that have no value for you or anyone else for that matter.

Your object of interest last night, the iron gate, could have the potential to lead to great trouble for many, including yourselves. I suggest you move on from your current interest in it.

Miss Lucy

It was time to pop the second bottle of Pinot while John went off to clean up. From the shower at Kokomo you can see the harbor below through a window that looks out onto the veranda. With a drink in hand I was sitting in a wicker chair just opposite watching him lather up his head when I asked him a question.

"What was that place and how did Miss Lucy know that we were there? Do you think she overheard us asking Judy about it? Or maybe that young girl mentioned to her we were asking about it. What has me wondering is how the hell did Miss Lucy, at her age, manage the steep decline from the road to the cottage and back?"

John by this point was out of the shower and dressing. He stepped out on the veranda and sat down across from me. After a short sip on his drink he began to talk.

"I find this whole thing a bit strange. After all, we are on this island for less than two days and already we are snooping around and being caught. Now we have this old island woman telling us to beware of asking too many questions about a rotting old gate off the road. Something is fishy about all of it. I don't know about you but maybe we should forget about the whole thing before we end up involved in something that we have no business being involved in."

I sat and listened to him and thought he had made a very good point. Without saying anything more we finished up our drinks and headed down the mountain to Shipwreck Inn our second favorite restaurant on the island.

Chapter Four

"Shipwreck Inn"

The Shipwreck Inn looks just like it sounds, a wreck. Its appeal is that it's one of the only restaurants facing the harbor at Coral Bay. Imagine a décor inspired by a collection of anything washed ashore that can be attached to a wall. The local patrons, like the dangling buoys, have that salty air about them and congregate at the bar. Those tourists who are brave enough to venture out from their "all-inclusive" hotels, generally sit on the porch facing the water. The first couple of years of going to Shipwreck Inn we were among the hotel set with one eye on the bar and the other on our Jeep. Now we feel comfortable enough to leave our keys in the ignition. This sense of security came from years of patronage and the friendly cook and owner Ellie. By experience we learned to stick to the basics on the menu like conch fritters and cheddar fries. If we are on a food binge we order the fries with brown gravy for an extra buck. Ellie calls us her honorary brothers and always welcomes us with a martini, up, no vermouth, and one olive. They were a welcomed delight after reading the note from Miss Lucy.

It was Ellie who told us about the legend of the Shipwreck Inn. She had inherited the place from a great uncle who she met once at Christmas when she was a very young girl. One day she received a letter from a lawyer on the island informing her of her inheritance. Single, and with nothing to keep her in the windy city of Chicago, she decided to check out her unexpected new fortune. When she arrived on the island the lawyer who had contacted her on behalf of the deceased met her and drove her to the place. After signing legal documents in his office in Cruz Bay, he handed over the key. Shipwreck Inn was now hers. The one stipulation in her great uncle's will was that she was not, under any circumstance to change anything about the place. She told us that when she first entered the place she felt a strange energy. It was neither scary nor friendly. It was a feeling that she wasn't there alone. In time, she became a self-proclaimed expert on the history of Coral Bay.

"You know there is more than what meets the eye about this place. It took me awhile to get used to it but now I'm fine. Back in the days of Blackbeard and his gang of pirates, this location was a favorite meeting place."

Over the years patronizing Shipwreck Inn we witnessed Ellie telling the story about the place to anyone interested in listening.

"Yep, right on this very spot after a few days of looting ships, mostly the Dutch who were exporting sugar from their plantations, the tricky devils would roam the Caribbean looking for prey and once the ships were anchored inside Coral Bay they would attack. The bay was the perfect place to trap them, small passage into it and surrounded by hidden coves where the pirates would hole up and wait to make their move."

We did notice over time that there were more and more embellishments to Ellie's story telling making the facts questionable, however, more interesting.

"The pirates would all meet right here on this very spot where a few of the locals set up a hideout. Eventually it became known as Shipwreck Hole where the swashbucklers would drink till dawn and admire their booty."

As the legend goes, or at least per Ellie, some of the décor in the place came directly from their ships. However, even a bit more speculative, is that there were spirits from the past that inhabited the place.

"The first night I was here cleaning the place up I swear I saw a bottle of Captain Morgan rum move from one end of the bar to the other, almost like it was floating in air. I swear and so you know I hardly ever touch the stuff!" On a few occasions, I must admit that I too sensed them hanging around.

We grabbed two stools at the bar and waited for Ellie to take our order. We sat back and looked across the section of hotel patrons and enjoyed the harbor view. Below the bobbing boats in the water were the remains of sunken vessels from past hurricanes. After the sun set the skeleton shadows of those ships long gone appeared in the rising moon. The events of the day down at the beach house and finding the note at the cottage may have made the night atmosphere seem even eerier than in the past. What contributed to it, no doubt, was the red glow of the candles submerged in teardrop shaped glasses wrapped in plastic netting. Without ordering Ellie came back to the bar dropping off our cheddar fries with gravy. She stood for a moment with a smirk on her face.

"Heard you boys were back. Yeah, someone was asking about you two earlier this evening. He wanted to know who you were." The smirk disappeared from her face.

Suddenly we felt a bit alarmed. I told her that we arrived yesterday and wanted to know who was asking about us.

"Yeah I know that you were at Miss Lucy's place last night with Judy." She replied, ignoring my question.

I thought that Judy must have told her about us being back and hoped that Ellie wasn't jealous because of the choice of restaurants on our first night. Then I asked, "Did Judy stop by today?" To which she responded, "Nope, but I have a question for you if you don't mind." We leaned forward to hear what she had to say.

"What are you two boys up to?"

John took a sip of his martini.

"What are you talking about?"

Now it was Ellie that leaned into us and whispered. "What were you two doing at that beach today? Are you looking for adventure? Most people who know this island have enough good sense to stay away from there."

I took a sip of my drink and said, "We spent the day enjoying our time at the beach." She nodded.

"Oh really? The one beach that is off limits and not so easy to get to? You better be careful."

I asked Ellie what the big deal was about that beach.

"Talk to that man standing at the end of the bar."

Then she walked away and told the family waiting for a table by the door to sit anywhere that they liked. They took a table out on the porch.

We looked across the room and saw the man. John turned to me and said it looked like the man standing on the beach near the house earlier. Suddenly, like the bottle of Captain Morgan Ellie talked about he appeared behind us out of thin air.

"It's a nice evening, isn't it?"

We both turned to face him.

“Darker out there on the water than usual.”

“Yes, seems to be a Waning Crescent Moon tonight.” I said.

John flashed me one of his “where did you get that from?!” looks.

I made a mental note to tell him later that I read it in one of the monthly tourist magazines detailing the timing of the tides, I found in the island market.

“I know about the note you found tonight at Kokomo Cottage and I was hoping that you would be here tonight. I delivered the note earlier in the day.” He then sat down next to John at the bar. John asked how he knew that we were at the cottage. The man who was easily in his late forties, took a sip from a bottle of Red Stripe beer and answered.

“My sister Lucy asked me to deliver it and I read it before leaving it at the cottage. She said that you were at her place last night with Judy.”

The mystery of how the frail woman could have maneuvered the steep decline to our cottage was solved.

“My sister learned about your discovery of the gate from my niece Isabel who overheard your conversation at dinner. Now, I don’t like to bother with the affairs of others most of the time, but you two are friends of Judy, and Judy is my friend as well.”

We finished our drinks and ordered another round and included one for him. Then he introduced himself.

“My name is Samuel and we need to talk.”

As the night grew even darker the hotel crowd thinned out. Flickering candlelight animated the dangling ropes attached to rusted hooks on the walls. The crawl of what little moonlight seeped in from the old windows casted long shadows across the wood plank floors. In web like patterns faint light exposed the branded scars left behind from cigarette burns from one end of the room to the other in the old creaky wood floor. Shipwreck Inn at this hour took on an onerous feeling. After so many years visiting the island it was on this night that I discovered for the first time an old Dutch proverb carved into a piece of driftwood hanging on the back wall of the Inn.

Goats beware on paths ahead of the man who speeds in the dark of night uncertain of his destination.

Chapter Five

"Samuel"

We got up from the bar and selected a table in the back of Shipwreck Inn. Samuel began to ask us questions.

"New Yorkers on a vacation?" We both nodded yes.

"How many years did you say you been coming to this island?"

"This is our 10th."

"All these years coming here to St. John, Lordy, you two must really like it here. Me, I only go as far as St. Thomas which isn't very far at all."

We told him that we once looked at property not so far from his sister's restaurant.

"The land was just up the road. It had a great view of the water but at the last minute we decide not to pursue it."

"I know that spit of land, it's near Crazy Louisa. Everyone around here knows that Louisa is as crazy as they come. I think it is from having too much time on one hand and too much marijuana in the other." Although we had only met her once we laughed and agreed that he was probably right.

"I know the Kennedy family that lives nearby. They have that ramshackle of a place right on the beach. The Kennedy's been on this island a very long time. They are friendly up to a certain point. You are probably better off not being in that location. I think you would have ended up with a problem on both sides."

At this point we weren't quite sure where this conversation was heading. Samuel seemed to be warming up and we became more relaxed in his company when he changed the topic of the conversation from real estate to what was on his mind.

"You may want to walk away from me like you did with that spit of land next to Louisa, but please hear me out. You see, there are folks around here like the Kennedy's and my sister Lucy that would be happy with the salt air being the only thing that has the power to change the landscape around here. I don't want no trouble for myself, and I don't want no trouble for anyone else, especially for my niece Isabel. I have lived here my whole life, only been to St. Thomas, like I said a few times. There is too much moving about there. I like it here better with my past as part of my future. But something needs to be done for my Isabel. Her future has a different kind of past, a kind that we don't speak about." John and I leaned in closer as Samuel began to speak in a whisper.

"Poor Isabel. She doesn't know what it is, but she senses there is something not good. Something is not right about her past here and she is correct if you ask me. She doesn't remember too much about her past and my sister Lucy tells me to 'be gone with the devil' when I try to talk to her about these things. She says things might occur, things that 'God himself cursed long ago'. She feels that this curse will be our end. But I believe that without knowing your past you will not have a future."

We spent a couple of hours listening to him and each drink revealed more of his conflict.

"Without knowing your past there can be no future," is what he kept repeating.

Ellie came over to our table after she closed the two-burner stove in the kitchen.

"You boys spending the night here with the pirates? I can manage one more round for you but I need to get back to my place before the goats get in my way, if you know what I mean." John laughed. "Goats around here are like the deer up north."

Samuel nodded. "Okay, one more and then I gotta get back to Miss Lucy's and turn down the place before she wakes and starts beating the path looking for me." She served one last round and Samuel settled the tab.

"My treat," he said as he pulled money out of his pocket.

John and I drank up fast and we three headed out to the parking lot. Samuel walked us over to our Jeep and as we started it up the lights from the dashboard lit up his face. He leaned into the window and spoke.

"There is a lot more to tell you. I know my sister Lucy wrote to you suggesting you keep away, but if you're interested in knowing more about what you discovered today meet me just beyond the gate tomorrow night at nine o'clock. I'll make sure it's not locked."

Chapter Six

“At Nine”

We drove to the gate and parked our Jeep across from Easter Rock. It was just five minutes before nine.

“What are we doing here?”

“You know exactly why we are here.”

“What? Are you sure we should be doing this?”

“No, but we may like the adventure.”

“What’s wrong with keeping it a simple vacation?”

“Nothing, but we’re here so let’s go. What could go wrong?”

“A secluded beach in the dark on an island…oh nothing could possibly go wrong!”

“Are you sure it’s not too late to turn back?”

John never heard me ask the question, he was already crossing the road and on his way.

The gate was unlocked like Samuel told us the night before so we slowly began to walk down the path to the beach. The sky was moonless which made navigating our way even more of a challenge. John said to listen for the waves crashing on the shore and head in that direction. We moved very slowly, careful not to stumble on the broken branches lining the path. Towards the bottom of the path and off in the distance we saw a flash of light. We stopped in our tracks and waited.

"This way, over here, come this way," Samuel said. We headed towards the light assured by his voice that we were going in the right direction. We cut away from the path and into the brush, now thick with vegetation. I imagined it was the old road that we saw the day before from the beach. If it wasn't for the flashlight that Samuel held I am sure we would have been lost. After what seemed an eternity we were on a rocky path and saw a light coming from the house.

Samuel walked us to the front door of the house. It was obvious that he had gotten there earlier to open it up. He led the way in as we entered the house. It took a moment for our eyes to adjust to the dim light provided by a few kerosene lamps in the room. The house smelled damp. The sound of bats flapping nearby only added more drama to the night. Once my eyes adjusted to the light inside I saw a pile of papers on the large dining table with chairs neatly arranged around it. A breakfront lined with china and crystal was against the wall and laced with cobwebs. To the right of the front door was a kitchen with a backdoor that led, I assumed, outside. At the end of the room a staircase leading to the second floor.

"Let's go upstairs. I've cleaned it up so that we can sit and talk."

You could see from below there was a balcony and more lanterns dimly lighting the walls. Even in its deteriorated state the house seemed to have a stately character. Samuel gestured for us to go up the stairs. All this time John and I avoided any eye contact. I think it was because neither one of us wanted to suggest to our host that maybe this wasn't a good idea after all. Like checking out exits in theatres, I was trying to figure out an escape plan for us if we needed to get out of there quickly. At the top of the staircase a glowing fireplace helped to veil the musty scent from below.

"Please sit here by the fireside," Samuel said. "I am going to get us a bottle of wine and glasses." He walked into a room off the balcony. John looked over at me with an expression that I interpreted as stay alert!

Samuel returned and after pouring us wine asked if we would like to look around. I then asked to whom the house belonged. The question was ignored.

Across the longest wall on the second floor were floor to ceiling bookcases. They were still housing numerous decaying books with picture frames hosting molding photos interspersed between them. Mounted between the bookshelves were paintings and a variety of stuffed ill-fated glass eyed animals. In their decrepit state, they blended into the dilapidated interior. At one end of the room was a badly weathered large floor to ceiling mirror dotted with black age spots. The result of unwelcomed moisture. Off the balcony there were a series of bedrooms, one of which we were politely asked not to enter. The others were made up as if guests were expected, however the bed linens were rotting from a long wait. From the open window, you could hear the waves hitting the beach and in between, the sound of crickets chirping as the temperature outside began to drop. How strange it all looked, even stranger was how it all felt.

Samuel spoke.

"This was the island home of Dr. Julius Robert Oppenheimer."

"The missing letters from the gate, O P P E N H E I M E R." John said turning to me.

"My question answered." I replied.

Chapter Seven

"The Doctor"

Samuel took a seat across from us and began to tell us his story during which time he opened another bottle of Cabernet.

"It was so many years ago, I believe it was the month of October, that news had spread across this tiny island about the arrival of this white man. It wasn't because of the color of his skin that people talked. It was the way he suddenly appeared on the island. Families found it to be a bit mysterious that he arrived in the middle of the night. The only person that saw his boat arrive from St. Thomas was Jackson "Jacko" Thompson, who just happened to be getting up unusually early to fish. According to Jacko, this barge pulled up to the dock, tied up to a slip, and within an hour a Land Rover loaded with supplies disembarked and headed north disappearing into the darkness. No sooner was he home from his morning fishing and telling his wife about what he saw did she spread the news to her neighbors. By sundown almost the entire island knew about Dr. Oppenheimer's arrival.

It was a few days later that a second barge arrived and this time it was carrying building supplies. No one knew who this man was and even without doing a thing he created suspicion on this small island. Almost overnight it seemed this house we are sitting in was built. This only added to the island gossip. The only thing people knew about the land was that it was owned by a couple from New York City who rarely visited. The sudden appearance of a new house on the beach caused the locals to talk. There is a saying around here that when people try to go un-noticed that's when they are noticed the most." Samuel paused and then smiled.

"That brings me to my sister Lucy. That woman is always going on about people and their secrets. She says that secrets are the work of the devil and there is no room for the devil here on her island. No such thing as a good secret. Lucy was not happy about having the Doctor living on the island right from the beginning. Oh Lord, she would carry on every time I mentioned his name." Samuel then mimicked the voice of a high-pitched chattering woman.

'No room for the devil to hide out on our island, you hear me boy? No room for that!'

I think because we were a bit on edge, not to mention encouraged by the wine, we couldn't help but repeat it. "No room for the devil, no room for that!" He laughed then poured another glass of wine and tossed a dry log on the fire.

"Shortly after the Doctor moved into this house Jacko told me that I might find some work and to visit and introduce myself. Jacko got to know him because he was transporting building materials for the house from St. Thomas during the construction. I was a young man at the time but even so, Lucy objected to me coming to meet the Doctor. My sister didn't like the idea that I was thinking about going to work for him but she also knew that there wasn't much opportunity for a young man to earn some money and help their family. Besides, it beat working at the dock or going back and forth to St. Thomas to load and unload the cargo ferry." John asked him about his parents.

"What did your parents have to say about all of this?"

"My parents? No, it was Lucy who raised me."

"Didn't you have parents on the island?"

"Well, you see this is how it was. "

Samuel looked away.

"My mother was a young girl when she had my sister Lucy with a man that she never talked about. Shortly after Lucy was born he came back to collect some of the stuff he had left at my mother's family house. He promised he'd come back after he found some work and made money to support his family. Before he left, my granny made him marry my mother. He only did it because he was forced to, that's what my mother told me. And even though they were husband and wife he took off one night and no one saw him for five years. I was told that no one missed him much, including my mother. The guy did eventually return, but for the wrong reason. He was dirt broke and saw my sister Lucy as his meal ticket. He threatened to take her away unless my mother gave him money."

Samuel's voice began to grow weak so he stopped talking and took a sip of wine. We three sat there for a while listening to the rain that had started only moments before. It was now pitch dark outside.

"Well no need for me to go soft at this point. Let me finish this so that I can get on with the important stuff." I said it was okay if he wanted to skip it.

"I don't want to."

"Of course." I sat back.

"Why would I do that? This is where I become part of the story."

He smiled.

"Lucy's father is mine too. Seems that when he came to claim her he wanted one more time with my mother. Lucy told me when I was older that it was an awful night of yelling. After a long fight at granny's house he forced himself on her right off the back porch. Took her so hard that she passed out right by the door. I was told I was the result of that struggle and Lucy always said that I was the best thing that came from mama's rape by that good for nothing vagrant. Can you imagine that?"

Pausing for a moment he started to laugh.

"Well, that scoundrel was now heading towards the dock with Lucy in his arms. My granny, who had just gotten home from church saw him leaving with her. She had no idea that he was back on the island or that my mother was passed out in the back yard at the time. Well that little feisty woman started to shout at him to put Lucy down. She was still wearing her church hat, one that I'll never forget, a straw bonnet with three pink roses arranged on one side. Granny called it her Queen of the Maypole hat!" John interrupted him for a minute and asked:

"Is that the same hat that hangs over the door to the kitchen at Miss Lucy's?"

"The very same. Lucy said that it kept evil away from granny, and that it would do the same for her. She hung it there the day she opened the restaurant. So, where was I in the story? Oh, so Granny seeing a hammer laying on the porch of her house grabbed it and began chasing him down the road. He had no idea what was about to happen to him. Within minutes she was joined by the other churchwomen in our neighborhood who all heard the ruckus going on. They all came out with whatever kitchen utensil turned weapon they could find. He realized he was not going to make it off the island with Lucy so he put her down and ran for the next ferry to St. Thomas. People talked for years how the island women, hats and all, took up arms, everything from a rolling pin to a meat fork, and chased this excuse of a man off the island. I loved that the church women were all wearing their Sunday hats while they were on the attack!"

Suddenly we began to look at Samuel differently.

I sensed that he wanted to take a break so I stood up and started to inspect some of the items on the bookshelves. Knowing more about who owned the house we took a closer look at the photos on display. I could identify the Doctor in some of the photos, after all he was infamous for having invented the Atomic Bomb.

Samuel poked the fire once again and began to speak.

"After a while life in our house returned to normal. I was about 10 years old when my mother met a man who was from St. Thomas. He was a friend of my aunt who moved there after she got married. He would visit from time to time and shortly after meeting her he proposed to my mother. Then there was talk on the island about why they wanted to get married in a hurry. But the church wouldn't allow it, given the fact that my mother was already married to a man that left her years ago. It wasn't much later that my sister Simone was born. People say that she is only my half-sister, but I never felt that way, plus mama was having enough trouble without us feeling conflicted about this little baby. She was named Simone. She was prettier than most babies I'd seen up until then, but it didn't matter, her birth created a whole lot of trouble for my mother. Even before the baby was born the man from St. Thomas stopped coming around and my mother refused to leave the house, not for anything."

We were captivated by Samuel's history as it unfolded. John asked if he wanted to talk about something else to which he said no.

"My mother died from grief, at least that is what I was told by my Granny. It was too much for her to handle, between the men that disappointed her, and friends that rejected her over time." I asked who raised him.

"After Mama died Granny cared for us until the good Lord called her to rest. That's when Lucy took charge, and believe me she thinks she still is! She was acting like a mother at a very young age, maybe a reason why she never cared much about marrying and becoming one. Simone never knew her mama because she was still a baby and too young to remember much about Granny too. Well, I guess all of this leads me to the point of asking you here tonight.

When I first started coming to this house, the Doctor was very slim, 'skinny like a fishing pole' my sister Lucy would say. She said that he did not have a look of health about him, maybe from drink and smoking I suppose. She was always reminding me to watch myself and not to be poking in anyone's business, especially his after I started working for him. Lucy left me alone after a period and expected me to come home every Saturday for dinner and church on Sunday. She told me if I missed dinner and church even once, she'd come after me and make a fool of me in front of everyone, by that she really meant the Doctor. I was able to avoid that because he was kind enough to give me time off on Saturday and Sunday so that I could keep my promise to Lucy." John then asked what kind of work did he do for the Doctor.

"Sometimes I would be clearing land around the house or fixing the tiles on the roof that had fallen below. There was a lot to do to keep the house up, especially a house like this with wood trim sitting so close to the salt water. After a while I took over duties as the cook and even learned how to drive. The Doctor taught me so that I could run errands and pick up supplies. Over the years there I would sometimes be asked to sit and have supper while we listened to music that would come from this radio he called a shortwave. Sounds from places far away and in languages I had never heard and the good Doctor would pull down a book from right there on that shelf and show me on a map of the places where the voices would come from. He would show me pictures of the cities and talk about the people who live in them. I would listen until it got dark and then I'd light these kerosene lamps to move us into the night. The Doctor, all this time, was alone. No one ever visited him. I think besides some of the merchants by the dock I was the only person he saw day to day. I'd sometimes watch him walk to the shore looking up at the night sky then bend down to the water and wash his face. I got the feeling he was trying to cleanse away a bad feeling."

I detected a warm tone in Samuel's voice towards the Doctor.

"I sometimes felt that I was the only person that the Doctor spent any time with during the first 6 years of working for him. But that changed and you'll understand better what I mean about the past having a lot to do with the future."

John asked Samuel if the Doctor ever talked about his past.

"No, never a word about where he come from or where he'd been. I wasn't all that interested either. He treated me good and never asked me questions about anything and in fairness to him I never did either."

John and I smiled as he went on with the story.

"So, you see Simone sometimes would come to meet me at the beach house on Saturday afternoons. She was now 16 and growing up. I don't think she ever told Lucy about it and neither did I because I liked her company. She would wait on the shore for me to finish my day's work so we could walk together back to Coral Bay for supper. Back then I was Simone's only male companion. My sister Lucy made sure no man would come around to pay her a visit. I knew that Simone needed company more than Lucy and me. During our walks to Coral Bay Simone would ask too many questions about my time here with the Doctor but I didn't care for there wasn't much other than that to talk about with her. Simone finished school when she was 17 and left the island for St. Thomas where she got a job working as a secretary for a construction company. Lucy was fine with it knowing that she was living with my cousin. But like she did with me, insisted that Simone make it home for the Saturday night dinner and Sunday church services. It was at church services that Simone shined. Her vocal talent was appreciated by the entire congregation, even Lucy was proud when my sister sang solo.

Simone began to take on the ways of those women on St. Thomas, wearing lipstick and using sweet smelling perfume. As she got older she looked more like the picture of my mother. My older sister Lucy never looked like that, never. Hell no! I guess she had the misfortune of looking more like our deadbeat father."

At this point we were on the edge of our seats waiting for Samuel to tell us what happened next.

"Then one Sunday after church she walked me back to the Doctor's house before the ferry ride back to St. Thomas. I left her on the beach while I gathered branches for the night's fire. I turned around to look for her when I saw the Doctor coming out of the house. He noticed her walking across the white beach in sunshine."

I looked over at John to see his reaction, the reflective flames from the fireplace flickered across an intrigued expression on his face.

"I walked back towards the two and introduced my sister to the Doctor." This time it was Samuel who got up and walked over to the bookshelves. He picked up a framed picture of a young beautiful woman laughing and holding hands with Oppenheimer and handed it to John. The woman in the picture was Simone.

Chapter Eight

"Oppenheimer House"

Samuel told us, using Lucy's expression, that 'things seemed to be moving on with the wind.' By that he meant happening fast.

"By this time, I figured out that she and the Doctor were seeing each other which was most likely the reason she decided to come back to St. John. Simone got a new job at a contracting office over in Cruz Bay. My sister Lucy, who hated secrets and was nobody's fool, knew that something was up. She began acting crazier and crazier every time Simone would come home late. After only a few months she made it impossible for Simone to live in the house. There were times that Lucy would cause such a ruckus with her screaming and yelling that I imagined the skeletons in the cemetery across the road were turning over to face down hoping to get some peace!

Simone never had to tell me what got Lucy whirling around in fits of crazy. I already knew it was all about the

Doctor. One night Simone said she had enough of Lucy's yelling and left the house telling us she was moving in with the Doctor. That was the night that everything changed."

Samuel told us that at first it was strange to have Simone move in with the Doctor.

"She moved into the spare bedroom on the second floor. I remained in the one downstairs behind the kitchen."

The room on the second floor was the one we were told not to enter earlier in the evening. He told us he was worried that they were getting romantically involved which would only lead to problems on the island. Not only was the Doctor a white man, but he was a great deal older than his little sister.

"Oh yeah, it was a fiery time all around at Lucy's house and now with Simone moving in things were changing at the Doctor's house. It was strange in the beginning to have Simone and me living together with the Doctor. Me, I was still single with not much of an interest to be involved. I guess I just hadn't found the right person or was too busy to look or maybe just not interested. My sister Lucy told us she would have nothing to do with either one of us. Life at the house fell into a routine, me working the grounds and Simone helping with the cooking and housework. At night, we'd sit with the Doctor and listen to the radio after dinner. After a while I would make an excuse that I need to take a walk or get some rest and let them be. I knew then as I did on the beach the first time they met. I knew.

Weeks went by and everything seemed fine until one day I found an old newspaper clipping tucked behind a row of books that read:

> *Dr. Oppenheimer, the inventor of the Atom bomb that decimated thousands of lives in Nagasaki and Hiroshima Japan in 1946 has been dismissed from the Commission on Atomic Energy. Asked about the devastation to humanity Dr. Oppenheimer responded: "As God is my witness I never imagined the extent of this destruction and I ask Him for His forgiveness before all of you present."*

I didn't bother to read the entire thing because I already knew that the Doctor was involved in this activity. People on the island had talked that he was the same Oppenheimer that was part of the creation of "the bomb" as it was referred to here on the island. But that day there was something that made me feel a bit uneasy reading about it there in his own house. It's when I decided to leave.

I was confused about a lot of stuff. Simone living there with the Doctor and me feeling like my life was not going anywhere. Don't get me wrong, the Doctor, nor my sister, never made me feel unwelcomed. It was just something down deep inside that made me feel it was time to leave and start a life of my own. When I left the house, it occurred to me that maybe the Doctor living so quietly on the island was hiding from something. I guess it was my own dark secret knowing that something just may not be right. Living with a man that invented a bomb that killed so many people. The same man that my sister was now living with. I began to think that my sister Lucy might be right about the work of the devil. I never shared that with anyone until now."

Samuel told us that he never found Simone that night to say goodbye. He wanted to talk to her and tell her why he was leaving but never had the chance to.

"I walked the beach looking for her then decided to head back to Coral Bay. Maybe I am the one, looking back on it all, that should feel ashamed for not talking to them that night, the only thing I could do was leave Simone a note."

Samuel never mentioned to us what he had written in the note. He did go back to the house a few days later to confirm that what he had heard was true.

"Apparently, my sister and the Doctor didn't stay too much longer at the house after I left that night. Jacko, who always seems to know the comings and goings on the island, saw them leave on a private boat two days later. I made it back to the house to confirm what he had told me and while I was there collected my personal belongings. The house was left in perfect order. Locking the door I headed back to Lucy's place. I guess you could say that I wasn't quite ready to be on my own."

Chapter Nine

"Simone"

The Villa Duc de St. Simone is an appropriate name for the hotel they moved to. It's a very private and elegant property in Paris where Simone and the Doctor took up residence when they decided to leave St. John. The hotel was located on the Left Bank in an area called Saint Germain. After Samuel's departure, the Doctor had asked Simone if she would like to move to Paris where they could live a more open life and that is what they did.

"You will love it Simone. So much to see and do. I should have thought about it long ago. To be away where no one will judge us and we could live freely. You know the French never think twice about an older man with a younger, beautiful woman. In fact, they see it as a badge of honor for both of us." The Doctor smiled while Simone laughed. But despite the lightness of his remark Simone was concerned about Samuel.

"The note from Samuel has me confused. He wrote telling me to be careful of my future given your past. What does he mean by this?"

The Doctor took Simone's hand and began to explain what it was that led him to St. John and why finding her had given him a renewed interest in life.

"My dear Simone, there is so much that I can tell you, but all of it is in the past. I'd like a fresh start with you hoping that you will understand."

Nothing more was said by either person and Simone, while terribly missing her brother, knew that in time things that were meant to be, would be. The reality was that Simone already knew about his past and living with him all these months never believed his discoveries meant to harm anyone.

Simone who had never been further than St. Thomas was now learning French and attending culinary classes. He ensured that she had the best tutors for both. She began to visit the sights on her own and found her independence as exhilarating at the exhibits on display at the Louvre.

He resumed some of the research he had started just before he left St. John. They would often meet at a romantic café in the early evening to exchange stories of their day. The Doctor would encourage her to speak in French and Simone would use it as an opportunity to tell him about how she had learned to make the perfect soufflé.

"Ne jamais manger un soufflé seul. Ce serait trop triste (Never eat a soufflé alone. That would be very sad)."

He would laugh and repeat what she had said to which they both agreed to never eat a soufflé unless the other was present.

"My dear Simone, what did you see at the museum this afternoon?"

"Well of course all of the required masters, da Vinci's Mona Lisa, the sculpture of Venus de Milo, and a very old but funny painting of two sisters. I think one was a Duchess, in which one of the women is pinching the other's nipple."

Simone and the Doctor had fallen deeply in love. They had been living in Paris for almost two years leaving behind their island isolation. In contrast to their time together on St. John, being in Paris was a very different time for them both. Simone told the Doctor. "I never imagined that you had so many friends." In response, he told her that they were more like acquaintances that he had met over the many years he was working, and more recently people he knew from the university.

"They haven't seen me in a long time so when people heard I was now living here in Paris they insisted on a night out. I hope you don't mind it too much, and truthfully I think that all they really want is to meet you."

Simone was delighted by the number of people in their circle in contrast to their rather secluded existence on St. John. When the conversation turned to the topic of scientific discoveries she tried to understand as much as she could. What she didn't understand she would ask the Doctor to explain when they were on their own. There were times that she found the conversation to be totally confusing and yet she would take the time to listen. She was in love and trusted him completely. Life was wonderful. As time sped ahead Simone was with child.

One late afternoon, Simone was thinking about home and the people and things she left behind. One of them was the scent of flowers in the salt air. Simone told her maid Anna how she missed the little Jasmine flowers that grew on the island and had the scent of the sweet salty air. The combination of scents made her very happy. She said to Anna, "A delicate white flower that offers so much delight. I wish I had some to wear in my hair".

"Je vais voir si je pouvais trouver (I will see if I can find it)," Anna told her.

But it was the Doctor who heard Simone speaking from another room and made certain it was found and delivered to her the next afternoon.

"Madame, look what was just delivered for you. It is Jasmine. It does have the scent of a tropical island." Anna then passed the box and card to Simone. She read the card and then held the flowers up to her face to smell. She was beaming. In the box containing the flowers was a note expressing his love and devotion and most surprisingly his plan for them to return to St. John. They had discussed the importance of their child being born there. For Simone, it seemed like the right thing to do, after all it was her home. However, the Doctor saw it in a more practical way. He wanted their child to be born on U.S. territory and given his legal address was still St. John it would be recorded as the child's place of birth.

They decided to go out and celebrate that night. Simone told Anna that she wanted to wear something very special, something that would complement the flowers that had arrived moments earlier.

"Yes, Madame, white from the House of Dior, or black Chanel?" "Oui, white from Dior is perfect with the flowers in my hair." Simone replied.

"Where are you and the Doctor going?" Anna asked and Simone answered. "The Café de la Paix, of course." It was their favorite place in Paris. There they spent many nights among friends, many of which were colleagues of the Doctor and becoming new friends for Simone. When they arrived at the cafe they were greeted by the maitre'd.

"Oh Claude," Simone said as they entered the restaurant. "Il est tellement agréable de vous revoir (It is so lovely to see you again)." They kissed on each cheek beginning on the left and then to the right.

"Simone, you look so lovely with the flowers in your hair. Jasmine, no?" Claude then showed them to their table in front of the house. Moments later when Simone got up to use the powder room, Claude saw it as an opportunity to approach her.

"Madame Simone, how are you feeling?"

"Wonderful. I only have a few more months before I'm due."

"Je suis content pour toi (I am happy for you)."

Simone then took him aside to tell him that she and the Doctor would be returning to St. John for the birth of their child.

"I see, but is it safe for you to travel with child so near?"

"Yes, we must, as it is important that the child be born there, per the Doctor that is. He feels that our child would have a healthier upbringing on the island versus the city, at least for the first few years. The second reason I am not too sure I agree with. He feels that it would be important for our child to know my roots, where I am from. He is no longer in touch with his family and feels that it is important for our child to have a sense of what it is like to have one. The one thing that I am excited about in returning is seeing my brother Samuel. I haven't seen him for a couple of years and miss him. He is my older brother."

"Que les anges veillent sur vous et vous guider vers toute securite," (May the angels watch over you and guide you back safely), he said and then asked if she would sing a song.

"Just one so that we will remember the sound in our hearts until you return." Simone blushed and waved him off.

When Simone returned from the powder room, and even before she took her seat back at the table, Claude was at the microphone announcing that she would grace them with a song.

Simone smiled and shook her finger at Claude in a playful manner before she approached the piano to sing.

She spoke to the pianist then looked over to the Doctor seated in front of her. Her choice, "Baby Mine."

The significance of this song's lyrics was appropriate for the story that was unfolding…

Baby mine, don't you cry.

Baby mine, dry your eyes.

Rest your head close to my heart,

Never to part, baby of mine.

When she finished, the Doctor stood and blew her a kiss. He then extended his hand to help her down from the small stage. They sat for a while and enjoyed one of their last evenings out, at least for a now, at the café.

The night ended with a walk along the Seine and across the Passerelle des Arts by the Louvre. Walking arm in arm on the narrow cobblestone street they reached the hotel and when they entered the courtyard he asked Simone to sit with him a moment. The moon was full and he reached inside his jacket. He placed a Cartier red leather box in her hand and said, “Si jamais, a chaque fois, pour toujours, (If ever, whenever, forever.)”

After they kissed she opened the box. Inside it was a crystal vile on a pendant with a diamond encrusted cabochon. It contained a powder blue substance.

“How beautiful, I recognized the contents too”

“Of course, my dear. It has the mystical powers to change things for the good. One never knowns when one might need it.”

Chapter Ten

"Redemption"

Samuel returned to the beach house immediately after he heard Simone was back on the island. And this time he didn't need to hear it from Jacko, everybody was talking.

"Like I told you earlier there is nothing that goes unnoticed on this small island. People were talking about the fancy boat that arrived at the dock and word spread like wild fire that Simone and the 'white Doctor' were back".

When Samuel went to see Simone, all seemed to be forgotten. The doubt and concern was washed over by the joy of their reunion.

"Are you sure the Doctor will be okay with me moving into the house?"

"Yes, of course. I think he missed you as much as I did. You should know that I talked to the Doctor about your concern and he understood, but asked that I trust him in his desire to make a new life and find redemption in the process."

"I am sorry that I judged him but I was only looking out for my little sister."

"I know. It is something that you've done all your life and I love you for it."

Samuel knew that there would be a whole lot of talking about Simone's return and more so about her pregnancy. It was obvious. He told us that she was due in a matter of weeks.

"Lordy, wait until Lucy finds out you're back and that she is going to be an aunt! It may just kill her."

"Let's hope not. We don't want to be blamed for that!"

I did apologize to Simone and the Doctor several times the first week that they were back on the Island. Each time they told me it was fine and that it was in the past now.

"Samuel, please there is no need to apologize. I understand now how it may have shocked you that I was involved with the Doctor. I know down deep that you were only looking out for your little sister. The Doctor and I often talked about you, what a good person you are, friend and brother, we realized this was something that took you by surprise."

Everything between them was forgiven as Simone proceeded to tell him about her adventures in Paris. It was as if nothing changed between them and he was relieved. They both were.

"That was so like Simone. She was so kind and said that she shared some of the responsibility for the situation. The next thing I knew is that she was talking about what she learned in Paris and her time learning about the art of making a soufflé. We doubled over with delight." Things got serious one evening when she told him about being with child.

"The Doctor and I are so happy that we are having this child. He needs to heal from deep-rooted guilt that he carries inside. The birth of a child, his child, may be the beginning of that process."

Samuel asked if they were married.

"Of course. It was a simple ceremony with just a few friends that we made living in Paris. My maid, Anna stood in as my witness, and the Doctor's oldest friend Mr. Kiko Foo was there for him. We thought it was important to make it legal."

John asked how she really felt about the Doctor's past?

Samuel said that Simone told him that the Doctor sometimes had terrible nightmares. "Shadows of death surrounded him". She believed that she was his vessel to forgiveness and that the child inside would be his redemption. Samuel continued to tell us what life was like after their return. It was getting late when I got up and walked to the window to close it. The rain had stopped and the temperature had dropped just as the sounds of crickets had earlier predicted. Samuel told us that for the next month they lived in anticipation of the child's birth. The three of them were having lunches on the beach then retreating to the library at dusk to listen to the radio before dinner. He told us that "peace enveloped the house".

"We did from time to time talk about Lucy. Once I moved back to live with the Doctor and Simone, Lucy stopped talking to me. She told me that I was the devil's fool and I better not come crawling back to her any time soon. Of course, as much as Simone wanted to see Lucy she knew that her older half-sister didn't want to have anything to do with her".

Samuel remembered a night at the house that he thought was amusing if not a bit odd.

"Cooking was now in the hands of my sister Simone. She had advanced from island cuisine, now being skilled in the art of French cooking having lived in Paris. When it was just me and the Doctor living here, I did most of the cooking. It was better that way since the Doctor had little interest in being in the kitchen. But every now and then I'd find him in the kitchen with Simone working on something. Most of the time he would ask her to watch what it was he was doing. I'd observed the two of them from the kitchen door that led out to the patio. He would tell her to monitor the thermometer closely and when it reached a certain temperature to add a powder substance."

John asked what was the powder he used.

"It was Laramar, a semi-precious stone found only in the Caribbean. I'd watch the Doctor take the stone and crush it up into a powder. I wasn't sure what it was they were trying to make. The funny thing is that they would always start with salt water gathered from down the beach but after they were done the Doctor would pour the water once it cooled on the plants in the garden."

"You mean he was taking the water from the sea and using it to water the garden after he boiled it on the stove?"

"That's right. When I asked about it he told me it was something that he had worked on long along. It was a process he discovered while working at Columbia University that involved a simple set up, select ingredients, and the right temperature to remove impurities thus making it safe to use in the garden. I thought that the Doctor was trying to teach her something important. He had handed Simone an envelope that he said had the directions written down in case she ever needed it and to keep it in a safe place. He told her that someday it might come in handy.

She never opened the envelope since the recipe seemed to her pretty simple. Simone folded it and placed it in the recipe box that once belonged to our mother."

John asked what he thought the Doctor was trying to teach Simone. Samuel said he never bothered to ask. He was just happy they were all together and Simone would soon be a mother.

"One night, Simone and I sat alone on the front porch when she said to me that it wasn't going to be an easy situation for us once the child was born. She asked me that night if I would do whatever necessary for her child. She wanted to be sure that the child was loved and protected if anything should ever happen to her. She knew even then that this wasn't going to be an easy time for her or the Doctor and made me promise that I would do right by the child. I thought it was a strange thing for her to say."

Samuel explained that it was late on an October night when Simone took to her bed. The Doctor was in the library listening to the shortwave radio while he was in the kitchen making tea for them. The storm, without a warning, picked up on the western side of the island.

Samuel said that he ran to the front of the house that faced west and began to close the open windows and secured the wooden shutters for added protection. Before running back inside he discovered the doctor on the roof trying to secure the antenna for his shortwave radio.

"The wind was whirling about and I heard the tea kettle whistle blow, then a cry of pain from Simone's room. I yelled out for the Doctor". Samuel stopped for a moment as if to collect his thoughts.

"When I got back inside the house I ran to the bedroom where Simone was. She told me that she was giving birth and to go find the Doctor. Trying not to panic I ran back outside to get the Doctor. At first, looking up at the roof I didn't see him. Then I found him. He was lying face down on the ground. The Doctor was dead. The cry of new life was met with the silence of death as the two passed in the Caribbean sky that very night. I prayed to the Lord that the two souls met in passing to and from this island house." Samuel's voice was faint at this point. He bowed his head. I sensed he was feeling a heavy sorrow recalling the incident.

"I couldn't tell Simone that night what I had seen so I left the house in the storm. I was so afraid. I needed to get my sister Lucy for help. I knew that Simone wouldn't be happy about it but I didn't know who else to turn to. It was the worst thing I could have done that night. I left Simone alone and broke my promise to protect her child."

Samuel told us that the storm was much stronger than he was that night. He said, holding back his tears, that it was stronger than him in many ways. He drove down to Coral Bay to find his sister Lucy. He told her she had to come back with him to the house. It was a matter of life and death.

"Lucy, in a fit of anger said to me on the ride back to the house that there was no good to come from any of this. No good. Now the devil will take care of the bad time that you and Simone brought upon us. Lord, Lord, Lord, she kept repeating, 'make the devil be gone now and forever. No good for us now.' She told me not to tell anyone about this. 'Don't even think about talking to anyone and if you do it better be when I am put into my grave. Be silent from now until my bones are six feet under, you hear me? I don't want nobody talking about any of this here. All these years that I had to look after you and that girl and this is what I get. I won't have any more of the devil's doings from you or Simone. Now get me there fast and not another word from you tonight.' I drove like a bat out of hell, not because Lucy was going on all crazy, but to get back to Simone to make sure that she was okay."

Samuel and Lucy drove in the rain. The wind tore the top from the Jeep. Lucy held onto the seat and continued to mumble about the devil's doing. When Lucy entered the house where Simone had just given birth she told Simone that she brought shame on the family and must leave this island and never return. Taking the newborn away from her, Lucy wrapped the child in a blanket and left the house.

"Looking back at me Lucy said, 'take me home to repair the damage the devil's charm has brought us.' It was the last time I saw Simone.

It has bothered me for so long that my sister had her child taken away from her in that manner. I made a promise to Simone to protect that child, a promise that I did not keep."

We couldn't drink fast enough while listening to his story. For a second I thought to myself what did we get ourselves into?

"Would you like another glass?" asked Samuel.

"Please, but just one more."

It was midnight and we were having our last drink when I asked Samuel why he was telling us the story.

Chapter Eleven

"Surprise"

It was just after midnight when Samuel suggested that we head out. He got up and made certain the fire was completely out before extinguishing the lanterns around the room upstairs. There was a stillness outside, the rain had stopped and we could see the moon. Once we were outside he locked the door then we followed him up to the road. The walk back to the road was made easier by the moonlight which now washed over our path. The mystery about the house on the beach was solved. We got into our Jeep and headed back to our cottage.

"Can you believe that?"

"Wow. You can write a book about this."

"I wonder why he's telling us?"

"Me too. I wonder if we are being set up?"

"That crossed my mind too, but to be honest the story is so crazy and in the end, all he was looking for was someone to share it with."

"Who would ever believe this? I mean we are here to celebrate your birthday and have been spending the time roaming ruins and a mysterious beach house. I'm not sure how we can help Samuel."

"Yes, I know. Mysterious is the key word there, but what a wonderful way to begin a new year!"

"I like the way you think."

With only two days left on the island we decided to lay low and spend time at the beach near Kokomo. On the official "day", we celebrated John's birthday on the veranda with the Key Lime pie that Judy made. We never told her or Ellie about our clandestine meeting and we expected that Samuel didn't either. We were sure that he didn't wanted Lucy to know that he was digging into the past, especially with strangers like us.

That Sunday we were leaving with less baggage than we had when we arrived. This is another of John's many (yet endearing) peccadilloes. John will pack shirts, pants, hats, books, DVDs, and even artwork on one occasion, to leave behind for anyone interested. You like this shirt? By the end of the night you'll be wearing it.

"I thought you liked that shirt?"

"I do, but you know what Buddha would say, 'own nothing'."

"Really, you know what I say? Buddha doesn't shop at Barney's!"

Samuel came down to the dock to see us off the island early that morning. We said we would like to help him reunite Simone with Isabel but we weren't sure how we could but would think about it. He told us he understood but if we thought of anything to call him and then handed us his telephone number. We shook hands moments before boarding the ferry back to St. Thomas and walked the plank with our bags. I happened to look back and saw that Samuel was still there watching as the boat pulled away from the dock.

Once in New York we were back to our daily routine with one exception, the topic of Samuel.

"It's been a few weeks since we said goodbye to Samuel."

"What's your point?"

I was a bit taken aback by John's response.

"What's my point?"

"I know, you're right, I've been thinking about him too."

"You have?"

"Of course. I can't get that image of him standing alone on the dock as we departed out of my head."

"I know what you mean. I got the feeling that he was staring at us as if we were his last chance for redemption."

"Do you think there is anything we can do to help him?"

"Funny you ask. I've been thinking about something we can do that may be of help."

"What?"

John reminded me of the article that I had torn out of the newspaper many years earlier—the short piece about Dr. Oppenheimer and his association with Columbia University.

"I thought that perhaps we could do a bit of detective work over at Columbia. I mean, it isn't too much for us to do given the campus is only a few blocks from our apartment."

"Okay, and what is it we are looking for there?"

"I'm not sure, but I do have a feeling that it may lead to something or not. Either way it could be fun. Besides, I know how much you love libraries!"

"True, libraries and cafeterias."

So, two nights after the conversation we were on our way to the University library. John had a friend there who registered us as "visiting researchers" providing us with carte blanche to files and the likes. His friend, a Columbia professor, was also well versed in the art of researching, which helped enormously.

Night after night for two weeks we scrolled though miles of microfilm, now digital, learning more about Dr. Oppenheimer. What we talked about when we were not at the library layered more mystery into our pursuit of information. For example, why did it take so long for Samuel to do something about Simone's disappearance? It was nearly 12 years since he last saw her on the island. Her daughter, Isabel was now a young lady. Why hadn't she attempted to contact her daughter after she was taken from her that night during the storm? Was there something or someone that Simone was hiding from? She had the right to her child, not to mention to return home if she wanted to. It just didn't add up.

What we learned about the Doctor indicated that he was a genius. Of German decent he was the son of an immigrant who moved to New York and became successful as a textile merchant. Documents described the young Oppenheimer as a lonely child and brilliant at his studies. After graduating from Harvard, he spent time at Cambridge University, where he was remembered as an extremely sensitive person. Then we came upon something that Samuel never mentioned, or perhaps never knew. Oppenheimer had been married earlier to another woman. His marriage was well documented, both the joys and struggles. There seemed to be issues in the relationship, perhaps due to his intense work at Los Alamos on the atomic bomb. It was a period of professional triumph as well personal loss. The struggle may have been what caused him to retreat from both his career, and ultimately, his family.

We continued researching for a few nights when we came across the first bit of information that seemed to connect to Samuel's story. It was a transcript of a meeting that Oppenheimer had with a colleague, Dr. Wu. They were both invited to conduct experiments at Columbia University. At the time, we did not know that it was commissioned by the U.S. government. The document now on film was in a handwriting that we believed to be the Doctor's given his signature was at the bottom of the page. It was this part in the document that rang a bell:

The procedure (patent #29987653) to achieve the desired results begins with saline water heated to a temperature of 500 degrees Fahrenheit. Once it reaches this temperature add the ingredient (confidential) and allow the liquid to foam. Once this has occurred you can remove the beaker from the heat and allow it to cool before you test results.

Dr. J. Robert Oppenheimer.

This was about the closest we came to matching some information up with Samuel's story. We asked around the campus about Dr. Wu since he was mentioned in the transcript that we happened upon only to learn that he was no longer there. Once again, the two of us ended up feeling that we had not discovered anything other than the mention of a formula that was reminiscent of our evening with Samuel in the house on St. John. Later that evening I suggested to John that we give it up.

"Let's call it quits." I said to John one night walking back home from the library.

"Call it quits?"

"Yes, if you are afraid of running into Samuel on our next trip to St. John's then we won't go there for your birthday."

"Not go back there for my birthday?"

"Let's leave things as they are. Who knows, the whole thing may have been some weird kind of situation that we can put behind us."

"Not go back there for my birthday?"

"I know you like St. John but we can try St. Bart's. You know, something new." John did not respond.

Within a few weeks, I was off to Paris for business. John seemed to be obsessed with the idea of finding out more about the story of Simone and continued to research the few characters that we had discovered earlier on. Still there were no leads or even clues so I suggested to John that he join me in Paris, hoping it would change the subject of Simone.

Chapter Twelve

"Café de la Paix"

Leaving on American Airlines, the Edsel of aviation these days, we traveled in business class to the City of Lights. After we checked in at L'Hotel, famous for being Oscar Wilde's final stop, John tried unsuccessfully to pry the medallion of Oscar off a door next to us to add to our collection of hotel memorabilia. We have a drawer in the kitchen filled with hotel keys, and not the typical plastic disposable kind mind you. I had an afternoon meeting so after an expensive coffee at the hotel I changed and headed there. John, of course, did the fashionable trek to the Musee d' Orsay, Louvre, and Café Marley for a cheeseburger. We met later in the day at the Hotel Costes for cocktails before we went off for dinner.

"How was your day?" John asked.

"French, of course, and yours?"

"French too."

"How was your lunch at Café Marley?"

"Very chic for a $25 burger on a bun!"

John told me that the best dish on the menu at Café Marley, which by the way overlooks the I. M. Pei Pyramid at the Louvre, is their cheeseburger. I agree.

John said as he was lifting his martini glass and noted, "Did you know that the cheese on the cheeseburger at Café Marley is American cheese?"

"Of course." I said raising my glass as well.

"Was there the typical large crowd standing in front of the Mona Lisa?"

He nodded yes and mentioned how the tourists would line up to take a photo of not the painting but with them standing in front of it!

"I hear the funniest things when I'm observing that painting, mostly from Americans. Seems people are always so disappointed to see how small the portrait is. I imagine they expect it to be larger than life."

"You know I must admit, I thought the same thing the first time I saw it."

"Do you know what the best thing about London is?" John asked.

"Paris," I said referencing the quote from Diane Veerland as we toasted.

It was our first drink in Paris. Ordering a martini there can be tricky. I've learned that when ordering a vodka martini requesting it without the vermouth is very confusing for the locals. More times than not they give you the vermouth without the vodka. This occurs because in Europe a "martini" is confused with a brand of vermouth called Martini & Rossi, thus when one orders a martini you get vermouth. One quickly learns to request vodka chilled up with an olive or in some finer establishments an "Americantini!"

"Waiter, si vouz plait, Americantini, oui ? Merci…" We'll see what we get this time. Of course, the ordering is accompanied with a lot of hand gestures which I am sure only adds to their confusion. Gesturing what ingredient not to add generally leads to the opposite result!

John told me earlier in the day about a French nightclub he wanted to go to that evening not far from the hotel.

"I read up on the best cafes to visit just before we left."

"Why is this one a must see?"

"It's the real deal. Great performers, food and the place is outrageously opulent."

"I'm game."

After we finished our aperitifs we headed over to the Café de la Paix.

Opulent doesn't even begin to describe what we encountered. The room was a shade of scarlet red, velvet curtains with glistening gold fringe enveloped private booths against the back wall. The room was entirely lit by candelabras from floor to ceiling and the sensuous glow of light echoed off mirrored walls throughout. Tuxedoed waiters stood in the shadows with silver champagne buckets at the ready. I was waiting for them to break out in a rendition of "Hello Dolly"! It had to be on Paris's best dressed list.

John chose this café because he had read about its unique live music in *The New Yorker*. He always does the groundwork for finding the best and most interesting places. I am eternally grateful that he decided to join me on this trip, otherwise I'd still be at the hotel bar trying to explain what a martini is supposed to be. We chose to sit at a table nearer the bar, closer to the drinks I always say, and were seated just as the entertainment was about to begin.

"*Mesdames et Messieurs les Députés, Mesdames et Messieurs, ce soir, nous avons la chance d'entendre le don de chanson de…Madame Simone.*"

We laughed at the prospect that this was the Simone that Samuel told us about.

"Look. She's here, right before our very eyes."

"Mystery solved." We laughed then toasted.

"To finding Simone!"

With the little information that we knew about Samuel's Simone we thought she would never end up singing in a Parisian café.

The first thing I noticed were her long slender legs. With one arm by her side the other wrapped around the microphone stand she looked out into the audience who sat in silence anticipating her first note. She looked down for just a moment then began singing. Her voice traveled in soulful cords directly our way. Closing her eyes on certain notes as if to encourage them to never fade away. It was a mood created that signaled she was not singing to those gathered in the club, but to someone else far away. We were only there to observe her travel the distance. I was determined not to miss one note as she sang "My Funny Valentine".

I looked across at John and then to Simone and felt it was no coincidence that we ended up there listening to this woman sing. The only image we had seen of Simone was that of a young lady, however the woman standing before us shared a very strong resemblance. After she finished her first number she smiled and after thanking the audience in French repeated her appreciation in English. I was almost certain this had to be her.

"Do you think that's her?" I asked. John looked at me and nodded yes.

"Look at her elegant features, the young girl we met, Isabel, has the same."

I then thought as she began her second song that there was something about the look in her eyes that were soulfully scanning the room that reminded me of Isabel. Was it possible that this was the Simone that which Samuel was looking for? It all seemed too easy.

We ordered another bottle of champagne thinking that Simone would reappear but she never did. The room escalated into a gleeful intoxicated state, animated patrons blurring in to the sensual surroundings. Waiters roamed from table to table, serving refills and elaborate plates of food while tinkling ivory keys competed with the laughter contained in this Parisian jewel box.

John broke my trance. "What do you think we should do?" I thought for a moment.

"We may want to contact Samuel in the morning and tell him about our discovery." John agreed and we settled our bill and walked back to the hotel.

The next morning our attempt to reach Samuel was not successful. The operator told us that the phone lines on St. John were down due to a storm. She suggested we try back the next day. Unable to reach Samuel we thought it would be a good idea to return to the Café and try to speak to Simone that night.

After a day of meetings for me, and shopping for John, we met at the Café de la Paix that evening. We were certain that is was the same Simone that Samuel had told us about.

"What are we going to say to her if we get a chance to talk to her?"

"We will figure it out when it happens."

"You mean if it happens."

We went back to the club that night in the hope that we would see Simone. We talked about making a connection with her so that we might confirm our hunch that this was Samuel's sister. That night we were greeted by the maitre'd who recognized us from the night before and seated us at a table close to the stage.

Simone made eye contact with us during her performance. John raised his glass to acknowledge it. I, on the other hand, wasn't quick enough to grab my glass so I smiled. Her performance like the night before was magical. Beautiful sounds carried the lyrics that filled the room. Unlike her exit the night before she stepped down off the small stage and walked into the room greeting its patrons.

"Gentlemen, I have noticed that you were here last night, the food perhaps?"

"No, we love your voice," John said.

Oui la nourriture! (Yes, the food.) I said in my terrible French thinking that I was agreeing with John's answer. Tilting her head, she smiled.

"Then let me sing a song for you. What is your favorite song?"

John requested the song that she'd sung the first night we were at the café.

Simone said, "Ah yes, Listen to My Heart."

Simone returned to the stage and sang the song.

"Listen to my heart, listen to it sing, listen to the words, it wants to tell you everything..."

Afterwards, she returned to us at the table and we asked her to join us for a glass of champagne.

"Do you boys come here often and I do not mean the Café de la Paix."

"Yes, we do."

“And why?”

“Because there is no better place to be than Paris with someone you love.”

Simone smiled then asked what we planned to do while in Paris.

“Well, there is the Gallery Lafayette and of course the Le Masion Blanc and…” le blah, le blah, le blah.

We all laughed. John mentioned how disappointed we were to learn that one needed to make a reservation 3 months in advance to get into Le Jules Verne, the restaurant located in the Eifel Tower.

“Yes, the Jules Verne is most difficult to secure for lunch, more so for dinner,” she said. “Would you like me to make a call to see if I can arrange a table? Oui?”

“Only if you will join us,” I said. I couldn’t believe I had suggested it but as John has always told me, ‘Fortune favors the bold’. She smiled and then said, “Well, why not, I haven’t any plans and I think it would be nice to spend time out with New Yorkers like you.”

Simone used the bar phone and quickly managed to get us a table.

“We are all set dear boys, a window table no less!”

“A window table at the Jules Verne for tomorrow night at nine! That’s amazing.”

I quietly thought to myself, Simone must be the next in line for the honor of being “Marianne,” the national figure for the symbol of the French Republic, to have secured this perch of indulgence. Or perhaps, she simply knows the right people!

“We’ll pick you up?” John said.

“No, no, please. No. I will meet you there at nine.”

And that she did.

While John had described his previous experience at Le Jules Verne, nothing he said could have prepared me for what I was about to witness.

Arriving just before 9 PM we entered the restaurant through a private entrance. Here we were checked in and escorted to a windowed elevator used only by guests, and traveled within the interior of the tower up almost 500 feet above the ground. When we reached the restaurant the view of the city took my breath away, especially the twinkling lights of Notre Dame. We were greeted by a handsome gentleman.

"Madame Oppenheimer has arrived and is seated at the table, please follow me."

It struck me that Simone was referred to as Madame Oppenheimer. As we approached, the city lights glowed behind her.

"Bonsoir, heureux de vous voir tous les deux."

"Yes, indeed we are so happy to see you as well."

I was taking in the entire scene with the dramatic views just outside the floor to ceiling windows. The tower's iron lattice girders provided a web enveloping the magnificence within. What could have been a more perfect evening to be sitting in the Jules Verne looking over the entire city of Paris? The lights of the Eiffel Tower reflecting into the restaurant created a golden halo where waiters floated like angels in air. It seemed magical that we were there with Simone. It was our second to last evening in Paris.

Simone had a cool vibe that helped me to relax more in her company. We talked first about the typical fare of being in Paris on business and enjoying the sights and as the wine flowed we transitioned to more personal topics.

"I'm the youngest of six Bronx born, Irish, recovering Catholics and I can run very fast which is a quality of great importance for a delicate petal such as myself," John informed her.

He also told her that in his house it was the first one up for the day that was the best dressed. His reason for being up so early was thanks to his bed being the family room couch. To this day, John is a great conversationalist and a skilled entertainer. Her sincere amusement was childlike. I then went onto speak about living in Connecticut and the time my mother watched me from our kitchen conducting the hedges in the back yard in preparation to be a drum major. John added while we were laughing that on occasion in the recent past he too watched me leading the band. In a very short period of time we grew close, almost as if forces beyond our control had been orchestrating the night.

"You know, well, you wouldn't of course, that I am from the Caribbean." Simone said in a very casual tone.

"Which island?" I asked.

"Well I actually lived on two growing up, St John, and briefly on St Thomas."

There was no doubt that we had found our girl.

"Oh, of course, two of my favorite Apostles!" John blurted. I truly love John for those references as Simone laughed using her napkin to cover her face.

"I have been living in Paris for almost 11 years." Simone said and then took a sip of wine.

Quickly John responded, "Do you miss anything living here?"

I clutched the edge of the table waiting for her response.

"Well, of course, I miss my home and family."

"Do you ever go back to visit?"

"Not for a very long time, a very long time."

Simone's voice trailed off to almost a whisper. The momentary break in our conversation ended when desert was served. We then returned to the topic of St. John.

"We like to visit the island every year in March to celebrate John's birthday," I mentioned while taking a spoonful of my flourless chocolate soufflé. John looked over at me knowing that one of us was about to mention our chance meeting with Samuel.

"Yes, I enjoy waking up on my birthday there."

"We've been visiting the same island cottage for years." I added.

"This year, as a matter of fact, was even more interesting that those in the past."

Simone asked John why it was more interesting. It was then that he leaned in and told her about our discovery of the Iron Gate which led to our meeting with a man on the island named Samuel.

Simone's expression at first was that of interest, then discomfort. I felt immediately that the conversation may have come across as calculated. I was right.

"Samuel is my brother, you talked to my brother?"

"Yes, while we were exploring the beach we came upon the house."

"What did he tell you?"

"He told us about things that happened there and stories about you and the Doctor."

"Did you speak to my sister Lucy?"

"No, but we did have dinner at her restaurant with our friend Judy and met your daughter while we were there."

"You saw Isabel while you were eating at my sister's restaurant? Pardon moi, I must excuse myself and go now."

When we asked her to stay she stood up, placed both hand on the table and leaned forward.

"I find this all very disturbing."

Without waiting for an answer from us she turned and walked away. To all that watched her leave the restaurant it was nothing less than elegant.

"May I have a Americantini? Merci," I asked the waiter. "Make it two," said John. It was all we could say at that moment. After finishing our drinks, we took the elevator down and reaching ground level the lights on the Eiffel Tower somehow appeared greyish rather than golden champagne in the night.

Chapter Thirteen

“Deux-Margot Café”

The next morning, we went to the Duex Margot Café in St. Germaine, a rather popular place for locals to take a plain croissant or a pain au chocolat with black coffee. We were troubled by how our night with Simone ended. It had started out so well. Why didn’t we let her know earlier on in the evening about our meeting Samuel? We were so close to helping Samuel out without realizing it and now we wondered if we would ever get to see her again. It was not a good feeling especially after she magically fell into our hands.

“What did we do?”

John wasn’t ready with an answer and tried to distract me with a question about his new YSL sunglasses.

“You know this design is from their archives.”

I ignored his attempt to change the subject. He put down his glasses and spoke up.

"I think it was the mention of Isabel last night. After all, Simone hasn't seen her since she was born."

I nodded and said that I am sure it didn't help that I mentioned that is was while we were at Miss Lucy's.

"Can you imagine how she must have felt hearing about a daughter she hasn't seen in years from a stranger. I am sure the conversation around seeing her must have triggered some guilt that Simone carries for leaving her child behind." John took a sip of his coffee.

"We never prepared for the possibility she might be the Simone that Samuel told us about."

"I guess we should have thought it through beforehand."

"You're right. Neither of us thought about how the information about seeing her brother and daughter coming from two people she just met might have consequences. I feel terrible."

I took his sunglasses and closely inspected the lenses.

"These are nice glasses."

"I think we should go back to the café and try to speak to her tonight, don't you?" John took his glasses from my hand and I agreed to go back to the cafe.

"Okay that's what we will do."

I took the glasses from him and tried them on.

"They look really good on you."

"Thanks. I think I may just wear them today."

It was our last full day in Paris and we had no plans other than to go to the café in the evening. We decided to wander around the city all day. I find that walking in Paris is kind of a religion. You see so much beauty, beauty that awakens thoughts of how amazing life is. The only thing one needs to do is enjoy the time. After a long walk and lunch, we went back to the hotel to rest before our evening out. Sometime during the day, I ended up surrendering the sunglasses over to John.

That evening we walked to the club hoping that Simone would be there. We wanted to speak to her before we left for New York. Taking the long way, we crossed the river and passed the Louvre as we headed to the café. We thought it was the right thing to do on our last night in

Paris. As we walked I asked John what we would say to her.

“I think we need to just apologize for not mentioning our encounter with Samuel earlier in the evening or at least try to explain that we just weren’t sure she was Samuel’s sister and hope that she will understand.”

“Maybe it’s a good thing we never reached Samuel on the phone the other day. I mean given Simone’s reaction last night I’m not sure she wants to see him again.”

“Maybe she doesn’t want to even consider what she left behind. She may have spent the last number of years trying to forget it all.”

It’s something we never even thought about, but on the other hand what if she wanted to know more about what Samuel shared with us? Either way we hoped that we would see her and find out more.

We were at the café in time to be seated for the show. I got the feeling that Claude was expecting us as he sat us at one of the desirable tables near the stage. He then walked up the stairs that led to the stage to make an announcement.

"Mesdames et Messieurs, j'ai le regret de vous informer que la charmante Simone ne sera pas avec nous ce soir, mais, nous avons la sensation américains d'étape d'Evita, Terri Klausner à effectuer ce soir. (Ladies and Gentlemen, I regret to inform you that the lovely Simone will not be with us tonight, but do not be disappointed as we have the American stage sensation of Evita, Terri Klausner to perform for you this evening).

"She isn't here tonight." John looked over at me.

"That's not good. I don't think this is going to work out the way we hoped."

Before John could respond Claude appeared at our table with a bottle of Cristal Champagne and two crystal flutes. We looked at the expensive champagne glasses and knew that they were not from the bar. Along with the champagne were two sprays of Jasmine wrapped in sea grass on a silver tray. Claude, charming as ever, pinned the boutonniere to our jacket lapels then handed us a note.

Gentlemen,

I am hoping you will be at the Café tonight so that Claude could present this note. If you are reading this, I want you to know that my sudden departure last evening was because of an immediate need for personal reflection.

I would like to be able to explain more to you in person. If you can meet me later this evening and return the two glasses, I know you know they are not the typical bar champagne flute, I would be most grateful if you could come. You can ask Claude for my address when you are leaving the café.

I do hope to see you both again.

Simone

John tucked the note into his breast pocket just as Claude returned to our table and served the champagne. I had the feeling that Claude was in on this because of the expression on his face. Oh, that charming Frenchman smile.

Chapter Fourteen

"310 Rue St Honore"

Claude was more than accommodating in providing us with Simone's address and a car to take us to 310 Rue St. Honore. We were dropped off at her apartment door which faced the entrance to Place Vendome, the chicest plaza in the world. It is the same plaza to home the most expensive boutiques in Paris, along with the Ritz Hotel. He had carefully wrapped the crystal flutes in table linens, which kept them safe as we made our way to Simone's home. As we entered the living room we could see all of Paris from the windows that flanked both sides of the fireplace. Simone's maid, dressed in black with a crisp white apron with a border of lace, greeted us at the door and took the glasses from John. When she returned to the room she lit the fireplace then spoke in French.

"Madame Simone sera bientot ici", (Madame Simone will be here shortly).

And shortly she was, Simone's entrance was as immediate as her exit the night before. We stood.

"Gentlemen, please sit and be comfortable. I already know you two know how to greet a lady from last night. It is a sign of chivalry that unfortunately many have forgotten. Such a shame to lose this. Don't you agree, no?" Simone was now seated and continued speaking.

"I am so sorry not to be at the club this evening to meet you. I needed time to do some serious thinking. In fact, I've been doing a lot of thinking since we saw each other last evening. I am so grateful that you accepted my invitation, especially after my rather abrupt exit from the restaurant. By the way, how was the new singer?" We smiled. I thought how at ease Simone seemed to be with us in her home.

"I understand that she is quite the thing in New York. I am planning to see the Broadway singer Ms. Klausner tomorrow night and wish I could convince you to stay one more day." We smiled again. I looked over at John, he was sitting on the edge of the sofa.

"I am so pleased that Claude passed on my note to you. He is such a dear friend and has been for so many years. I don't know what I would have done without him. It is so, I wish I could find the right word, not funny but probably more than coincidental that you were at the café the other night. I think it is sort of a miracle that you ended up there of all places. Simone paused and gently wiped her eyes. We all took a sip from our drinks that the maid had served moments before. She continued speaking.

"This is better, no? We can talk here, or I can, it's easier in my own home."

Her casual tone was disarming. I wasn't sure where Simone was going with all of this. I sensed the conversation could go two ways, appreciation or something to the contrary. She then stood up and walked to the window that looked out over the plaza.

"Would you like a refill? Anna makes a superb martini, no vermouth is the trick, oui?" Simone called out to her maid who appeared and refilled our glasses from a crystal pitcher. When she left the room, Simone turned back to look out the window.

"I spoke to my brother Samuel today." Here it comes I thought and like John I was leaning into the room holding onto the sofa cushion beneath me.

"It had been a very long time since we spoke. In fact, the last time was when my daughter was born. I remember so clearly our conversation back then. I had asked him to make a promise to me. A promise between a brother and sister." She then turned and faced us.

"My brother Samuel is such an interesting person. I learned a great deal from him growing up on the island. Things like believing in oneself and always try to do what is right regardless of what others may think or say. Don't be fooled by the simple life he lives; he is not a simple man. In fact, I sometimes envy how blessed he is with his life, so knowing, and above all else, honest. My half-sister Lucy, well, she is not an easy woman to be around. I'll say that about her. Anyway, Samuel cried on the phone today. I found it painful to hear him cry while we talked."

"You spoke to Samuel today?" John said.

"Yes, I did and told him I met the two of you."

The silence in the room made me feel uncomfortable. I still wasn't sure where this was going. Was she upset that we had discovered her here in Paris or was her thoughtful day leading to a reconciliation of things from her past?

"He told me that he feared that he would never see me again. That, of course, changed after he met you two. It seemed your interest in his story gave him renewed hope that one day we would speak to each other again." John lowered his glass and spoke as I looked on.

"Sorry, we didn't mean to interfere with either of your lives."

"Please let me continue." Simone whispered, folding her arms in front of her.

"I think it is important for you both to understand my feelings. What's done is done."

John looked over at me making a funny gesture with his lower lip as if we got caught doing something we shouldn't have been doing.

"Just in case my brother didn't tell you everything about me. Back on the island growing up with the only people in my life being Lucy and Samuel I used to fanaticize that someday I would have many friends. That I would be able to see the world and do things that I could only read about in magazines left behind by tourists. It wasn't until I went to work in an office on St. Thomas that I began to realize that it could be possible. Seeing so many more people on an island so much larger then St. John helped me to understand that there are people who live so beautifully. They live differently. Just riding back on the ferry from Charlotte Amalie to Cruz Bay I'd listen to people talk about their journey leaving from New York, or wherever they were from, and arriving on St. John. I became aware that there were places beyond my home that I hoped to see one day." Simone then took a seat on the sofa opposite us. We too sat back on the sofa facing her.

"I was very young when I met the Doctor. At first I was sure that I'd be intimidated when and if ever I met him. When I did, it was almost as if I'd known him all my life. He was so kind that I felt completely comfortable being with him. Yes, he was much older but that didn't matter to me. It didn't take long before I was in love. I knew that this love would create turbulence at home, and Lord knows it did." Simone laughed. We began to feel more relaxed by her body language.

"I felt that not even the strongest storm could end the love that we shared. But ironically it did. My daughter, our daughter, was born the same night my husband died. I felt that I was being punished for my actions and I now realize that I have passed that punishment on." She stood and walked back over to the window. There was a moment of silence, but this time it didn't feel uncomfortable. It was a sense of relief.

"Lucy called the police that night to report the accident. After they took his body away I felt helpless. I sat in the house alone for a few days hoping that it was all just a nightmare, but of course it wasn't. I left St. John a couple of days later after trying to reason with Lucy to get my child back. She threatened me and told me to leave the island or else she would make trouble for me and the child if I stayed. 'You married a white man, and had his child. That child will suffer enough with people talking about how she is a mixture of black and white. If you don't leave this island fast I will, with the Lord's help, make you wish you never returned'. Those were her last words as she shut the bedroom door.

After his body was buried, I packed my things and came back here. He had provided me with the means to be independent early on and I am grateful. I had the resources to leave my past behind. But one never can really leave their past behind. I can hear my brother saying to me, 'your past is your future and your future is your past.'"

Simone used the exact same words Samuel did when we met that first night at Shipwreck Inn.

"I traveled back here to Paris. I wanted to try and pick up the pieces of my life, you know, begin over with whatever strength I had stored by the love that I still had for him. Although I tried to forget about Isabel I often wonder about my young daughter. While I have harbored a great deal of resentment toward Lucy's action, I know that Isabel is being carefully looked after. Once I was settled in back here I made little effort to contact her. My sister would have made it impossible, I told myself, a convenient excuse. I believe now that I may have even preferred it that way. I am ashamed to say that I thought that her birth may have been a curse. I lost the one man I loved and gave birth to his daughter at the same time. It wasn't an easy tradeoff for me to deal with."

Simone turned facing out the window and said in a determined voice, "It was irresponsible of me to do that."

John and I knew in a Maupassant moment that Simone sensed our concern and understanding of her situation. We felt that we were embraced by this beautiful and strong woman.

John then asked what she and Samuel talked about. Simone leaned forward looking directly at us and said.

"I told him that I never stopped believing he would keep his promise and you are the proof of that. Samuel told me that he was hoping that something would come from his meeting you. He explained how he met you and what he told you. He said he somehow had a renewed faith that things would work out after his evening at the beach house. Funny, I'm not one to believe in coincidence. But I do believe our meeting was meant to be and that the tragedy of my past is what brought us together. I hope that I am clear about my situation and please know that last night I wasn't prepared to discuss this."

Overlooking the Place Vendome from her apartment I had never quite seen it from this unique perspective. I felt a certain privilege looking at the view and seeing it with John and Simone. It was getting late and with our early departure we decided it was best to say goodnight.

"It was so wonderful to see you both tonight and share some of my life. Please travel safely back home. I will be in touch. I have much to do now. Bonne nuit, goodnight, we will see each other soon. Look at the beautiful lights of the city, Paris at its finest!"

As she was gesturing to the lights in the city I wondered if she saw the same dim lights as we the night before. The lights this evening were indeed beautiful. They were back to a champagne gold that shines on all those in love. We waved Simone farewell as we walked into the night.

Chapter Fifteen

"August Vacation"

"Look what just came in the mail." John was sorting through the pile in front of our door. "It's a letter from Simone."

After showing me the return address embossed on the back of the envelope he opened it.

My Dear Gentlemen,

I know that this may be a bit unexpected, but would you please join me in London? I remember that you said you take a summer holiday during the last two weeks of August, and hope that this is still the case. The tickets are enclosed. I know that this is a lot to ask and I will explain more when I, hopefully, see you. You must know that I am asking because I need your support.

Forever grateful,
Simone

P.S. I'll be waiting at the airport!

Inside the envelope were 2 first class tickets that Simone mentioned in her note. John handed them to me. "First Class tickets to London? What do you think this is about?" John shrugged.

"And what about our plans to go out to the beach?" John didn't answer and started to read the letter again.

"I wish it wasn't so cryptic. Why a letter and not just a phone call?" John said as he put the letter back into the envelope.

"Maybe we should give her a call."

When John attempted to speak to her he discovered that her phone was out of order so he immediately dialed Samuel.

"Maybe Samuel knows what this is all about."

He covered part of the phone and told me that it was ringing.

"Hello, may I speak to Samuel?" The voice on the other end asked John who was calling.

"I'm an old friend."

John stood listening hoping he would come to the phone. But instead the person on the other end asked what the call was for.

"I just wanted to find out about the property near the beach by the Kennedy family." Quick thinking, I thought to myself. John then looked over and rolled his eyes. I knew then that he must have been speaking to Lucy.

"Well if you see him, please ask him to call me?" There was a short pause and John mouthed that she said she was getting a pen.

"Yes, that's it, now it's important that I speak to him soon. You will give him the message? Thank you and goodnight."

John said he was almost sure that Samuel would never get the message given Lucy's tone on the phone. I told him we should try again and maybe we will get him instead of her next time.

"We can do that. I thought about calling Judy but I don't think Samuel wants us to share this, at least that's the feeling I got when we saw him",

We continued to try to reach both Simone and Samuel but every attempt ended the same way. Simone's phone was disconnected and Samuel was never home according to Lucy. We started to wonder if they were in trouble.

"You know this is all very strange. We get a letter with two airline tickets and we don't even know why. On top of that we can't get in touch with the person that sent them or her brother who got us into all of this." I nodded in agreement.

"Are we just supposed to pack up and go, forget about our own plans?" I nodded in agreement, again.

"So, you think we should go without any word from either one?" His tone was curiously innocent. I finally spoke.

"Yes, I think there is something going on. It's just this feeling I have that it's the right thing to do. Who knows maybe she purposely disconnected her phone.

"If that is how you feel then let's go." He then handed me the tickets.

Perhaps we were a bit premature in thinking that our adventure with Simone and Samuel was over. Just like our meeting at the iron-gate that night on St. John, we weren't sure what we were about to get into but we quickly rearranged our plans to meet Simone.

First Class on most airlines is swank but on Virgin Air it is total indulgence. There is continuous disco dancing down the aisles while the champagne and caviar flows for eight hours as you cross the Atlantic. Between sips we talked about what we were going to do while we were in London.

"You know I've never been to the Tower of London."

"Well, neither have I so maybe we should head there after we check into our hotel."

"Hotel?" I put my glass down on the tray between our seats.

"Simone never mentioned where we were staying did she?

"You're right, all she said is that she would meet us at the airport."

"Well I am sure we will be staying in a 5-star property."

"Yes, for certain."

"The one place I read that we should avoid at all cost is Madame Tussauds, I hear it's a waste of time."

"Fine by me."

"Good, if we were ever interested in wax figures there is one here on 42nd Street."

"If ever."

Once we arrived we quickly learned that we wouldn't even get close to Buckingham Palace.

"Bonjour Bonjour, hello hello, I am so happy to see you again! Simone said greeting us at the gate dressed in a white linen top and matching slacks wearing a pair of black Hermes sandals (I could tell from the buckle). We were then escorted to a VIP lounge nearby.

"I am thrilled beyond words that you're here." Simone then kissed us on both cheeks followed by a big hug.

"I knew you would come and I was so very touched that you said yes on such short notice. But first, please, a glass of champagne to celebrate our reunion and then I can tell you what this is all about."

"Simone, we were very concerned about you and your letter seemed so vague." John said as we were seated. I then told her that we tried numerous times to reach her by phone and we kept getting a busy signal.

"You shouldn't have been worried," she said.

"Yes, we were, and for days we tried to reach you, in fact we even tried to reach Claude at the Café de la Paix but got a recording that it was closed for the month of August. We also tried to call your brother Samuel but evidently the messages we left never got to him. What is this all about?" I asked.

"Oh, my dears, the phone, oh my, Je suis vraiment desole! I am so sorry! My phone has been disconnected for over a month now. I've been using a cell phone instead because of how long it takes for the phone company to come and repair it. I think they may have been on strike for the past few weeks, you know how it is in France. Oh my, I never wanted you to worry. I should have called instead of writing a letter. Please forgive me."

John looked over at me then said to Simone. "Why wouldn't Samuel return our calls?" Simone shrugged, then said that he probably never got our messages from Lucy.

"I'm not sure. I've spoken to him but he always has called me and he knows about my request to have you join me. If he didn't return your calls, I wouldn't be surprised if it's because Lucy never told him you called."

It was now making some sense, but we still didn't understand why we were in London sitting in the VIP lounge. As we started to relax John asked about her maid Anna. I looked over at him thinking why are you asking about her maid?

"Very sad" Simone said.

"I had to let Anna go after I caught her taking silver from the apartment next door when the unfortunate man who lived there suddenly passed away. I didn't think I could really trust her after that." John said we knew someone that did the same thing back in New York. I looked over at John then back at Simone and smiled. She took it as her cue to continue.

"After you boys left I decided to call Samuel to let him know how delighted I was that we were back in touch. It was during that conversation that he reminded me of something that had to do with the Doctor." Now we are getting somewhere I thought. I looked over at John when Simone began to explain.

"When I was speaking to Samuel he happened to mention a Dr. Wu as he was reminiscing about his earlier days with the Doctor. He told me that before I left that the Doctor had often mentioned his concern for his fellow colleague back at Columbia. I too remember the Doctor talking about Dr. Wu with great fondness. He once told me that he was the one person that he trusted after the situation that occurred leading to his exile from the scientific community."

John then told Simone about our amateur investigation into the Doctor and coming up with Dr. Wu in the process.

"After we got back to New York we went to the library at Columbia University to look up information about Dr. Oppenheimer. There wasn't a great deal on file regarding his career highlights and family background. There were notes between he and a Dr. Wu, whom you just mentioned."

"Do you remember the information?"

"Well," John said. "It was some kind of notation for an experiment."

"Interesting." Simone said. "Do you remember anything else about it?"

"Something about measuring the exact temperature, but it didn't really make any sense to me."

Simone smiled as a sign of assurance that she now believed she was on to some new discovery.

"He often explained that someday the work that he and Dr. Wu did at Columbia would be his redemption. I understood what he meant. He did tell me that one day Dr. Wu suddenly disappeared. He never showed up for their laboratory work."

Her tone seemed to be very serious at this point and her voice dropped to a whisper.

"The Doctor never went into details regarding what they were working on, only that it was extremely valuable. He carried great concern for the mysterious loss of his friend."

John then asked if she knew where to find Dr. Wu.

"I was just getting to that. After that conversation with Samuel I made a few calls to the Chair of Science Studies at Columbia University but they weren't much help. I was told that they had no record of where he went after leaving the University."

I understood the answer Simone received from the Chair of Science given the little data we gathered on Dr. Oppenheimer at the University library. It seemed odd that there was so little information on file or maybe the University was trying to keep things from being accessible. The only clue we had come across was a cryptic memo between Dr. Oppenheimer and Wu on micro-film. Who was it that she spoke to there?

"Even though I didn't get any information on Dr. Wu's whereabouts when I called the University, I realized there might be one person who could lead me in the right direction. I have an instinct that Dr. Wu may be able to help me answer a question that keeps running through my mind and I am determined to find out where he is."

Simone then poured us another glass of champagne and said: "I know that this is a lot to ask you both but would you consider traveling with me to Shanghai?"

"Shanghai?" I coughed on my champagne.

"Why Shanghai?" John asked.

"That's where Dr. Wu is!" Simone took a sip of her drink.

"I was determined to find out and I did!"

John looked over at me then asked what time was the flight for Shanghai?

Simone looked down at her Cartier watch. "In about an hour."

It was during our flight to China that Simone revealed more information about her motive for wanting to see Dr. Wu.

"There is something that he knows that I need to understand. This all goes back to a conversation that I had with him just before the Doctor died."

"How did you find out he was in Shanghai?"

"Many years ago, I met a friend of the Doctor's named Kiko Foo, he was a witness at our wedding. A lovely gentleman, very trustworthy. Over the years, I got to know Kiko and he proved to be a very good friend. He once told me if I ever needed help to contact him. I called him immediately after speaking to the Chair at Columbia."

"What was his relationship with the Dr. Oppenheimer?"

"They had worked together many years earlier in New Mexico and became great friends."

"How did he know where to find Dr. Wu?"

Simone smiled.

"His profession provides him with access to classified information."

"Oh, this is becoming even more of an adventure than we thought." I said, but there was more.

"Kiko has arranged a meeting to speak to Dr. Wu."

Simone told us that Kiko told her a meeting with Dr. Wu would require a great degree of discretion. The meeting would be highly confidential. He told her to be in Shanghai during the 2nd week of August

"Kiko told me he could pull this off. Timing had to be mid-August when the city is swamped with tourists celebrating the Hungry Ghost Festival throughout China."

He instructed her to travel with a couple of trusted friends to give the appearance that she was on holiday. While we still had no idea of what the meeting was for Simone assured us we were in good hands.

"So, all we need to do is act like tourists?"

"Yes, we will be traveling to see some sights, and discover the secrets of China, so to speak."

"Seems simple enough," I said. Or was it?

Shortly into our flight we all feel asleep. The combination of updates and champagne was exhausting. When we landed, two gentlemen dressed in black suits met us on the tarmac. They greeted us, took our carry-on luggage and led us to a waiting black Rolls Royce. We were told by one of the gentlemen in black that Immigration and Customs was already taken care of as we sped off on route to The Shanghai Grand Hotel. Approaching the city, everything looked so different. I had been there many years earlier.

When I was in Shanghai it was the early 80's. The roads were narrow and primitive and mainly dirt. Everything back then would drain into the river from the streets, rain, sewage and industrial waste. It was the only water source for the 5 to 7 million people living in the city. Even then some of the women were still wearing clothing from the 40's. After the 1950 revolution Western dress was not available. Most people were subjected to wearing Mao suits. This type of dress was more of a uniform which emerged during the Cultural Revolution. The unisex suit, mainly in grey was a simple jacket with five buttons down the front, four external pockets, and a turn-down collar.

China was under Communist control back then and Shanghai was a poor city within an even poorer country. As a young man, I was taken aback by the decay of a culture once so opulent. I was in awe of the remnants left behind of its past under British occupation. On this return that seemed to have all changed.

As we passed a fleet of luxury cars, a sign of modern times, on the road leading from the airport you could see the skyline of what now was a futuristic metropolis. Our driver told us that one fourth of all the building cranes in the world were now in Shanghai where high-rise glass and steel towers mushroomed upwards into the sky.

One thing that did not change was the grandeur of The Shanghai Grand Hotel which was built during the colonization by the British and had survived. Pulling up to the porte-cochere, we were greeted by a man in a grey morning suit who we quickly learned was the Hotel's General Manager. His broad smile was flanked by uniformed bellboys.

"Check out the uniforms, the hats, like something out of an old movie." I knew the moment that John said it he was thinking about how he would nab one to add to his collection of hotel memorabilia.

The General Manager took Simone's arm and escorted her to a private elevator as we followed.

"Welcome to The Shanghai Grand, Madame, so pleased to welcome you to China. Have you ever been to China?"

"No, my first visit here." Simone replied.

"I hope you and your gentlemen companions will enjoy the suite of rooms we have chosen for you. This elevator is for your personal use while you are in residence and you have your own security code to access the lift whenever you need it. The code is written on the interior of your hotel passport. Ah, Penthouse floor, here we are, please, after you."

"Merci beaucoup." Simone said as we got off the elevator.

In front of us was a set of double gold leaf doors that led to an entire floor of rooms for our stay. We not only had a full view of the river, but we could see it from every one of the six rooms on the penthouse floor. There were two master suites both with fireplaces and silk lined walls. This amazing décor inside was only to be further enhanced by a large patio and infinity pool made from blue lapis stone. The well-stocked bar on the roof of this grand hotel was surround by mirrors reflecting the city skyline. The bellboys escorted us into our separate suites while the hotel's General Manager stood by the front door.

"Are you comfortable in your suite?"

"Yes, quite, thank you," said Simone and the hotel staff departed.

"Thank you for being so generous with us on this trip." John said.

"No, it is I who recognized your generosity on our first meeting in Paris."

We were now settled into our room after hours of travelling. As we were enjoying the view from the patio Simone joined us. She was in a different outfit.

"Kiko knows we are here and I am going out to meet him at a restaurant nearby. I do apologize that I cannot take you with me but he wanted to meet this first time alone to discuss some of the details of this trip."

"That's perfectly understandable."

"Yes, we know that you need to catch up; we will be just fine."

"I promise that I will share everything with you when I get back from seeing him. Please enjoy the evening here or ask the GM to book a table for you should you choose to go out, and most of all, trust me, please."

Enjoying the luxury of our penthouse suite and the fully stocked poolside bar we decided we would manage nicely on our own.

When Simone left, we settled in at the penthouse pool bar after a swim. We put on the complimentary robes at the pool cabana and we decided to make a few drinks. It was now about nine in the evening and John put in a call to find out about dinner reservations.

"There is no answer."

"What do you mean there is no answer?"

"Just what I said, the phone line is dead."

Having discovered the hotel phone was not working we decided to take the elevator down to the lobby. After we dressed we headed to the elevator.

"What is the code to access the elevator?"

"Oh right, it's in our room passport."

"Do you have it?"

We both searched our rooms but could not find it.

"Did the GM give it to you?"

"No, but I know there were two in his hand, one for us and the other for Simone."

"Do you think it is a bit weird, no phone, no elevator code?"

Then the paranoia set in.

"Are we captive here?" John asked.

"Who is this woman and why did we trust her enough to change our plans to travel here instead of sticking to our original plans?"

John and I sat in silence, thinking.

"We are too trusting and look where we have ended up, captive in a hotel penthouse in Shanghai!" I said, heading back out to the poolside bar.

We sat at the bar and made a few drinks to calm our nerves. After a few hours, we fell asleep on the lounge chairs by the pool. Vodka is like liquid Ambien.

It was about midnight when Simone woke us up.

"Are you two okay?", she asked, glancing back at the pool bar and the lineup of glasses.

We could only look up at her at that moment in the hopes that we were.

"I am so sorry about the hotel passports. I had both in my bag all this time. The GM handed them to me just before he left us. I discovered them when I reached into my evening bag at the end of the night. I didn't intend to leave you here without them. I am so embarrassed."

We both sat in silence not quite knowing if the explanation for our containment could be so simple.

John asked, "What about the house phone?"

"Oh, my dear, all the phone lines were down at the hotel because of an overload. I discovered that after I tried to reach you to tell you that I had your hotel passport. Here, let me give them to you now so you will understand that you have nothing to worry about."

Simone poured a gin and tonic at the bar.

"I must tell you that I was concerned that you might think differently of me after this faux pas, but truly it is I who think differently of you. You are both very trustworthy, in fact, at my dinner with Kiko Foo, I explained to him that without you here I wouldn't be able to go through with any plans he made. He told me he needed to hear that directly from me in person so that he could feel comfortable as well.

"The plan?" I said.

"It is so late and I would like to talk about my night with Kiko, but I think we are all tired from our travel. Is it alright that we talk at breakfast?", Simone said as she poured what remained of her drink down the drain.

"Yes of course, until the morning. Good night."

John took our hotel passport and we took our remaining drinks back to our suite. At about 4AM we got up to see if our passport code would access the lift. We were relieved to find it worked. Back in bed, John asked me what I thought the plan was?

Chapter Sixteen

"Shanghai Breakfast"

John and I were having coffee by the pool the next morning when Simone joined us.

"Did you sleep well? As best you could under the circumstances? I am so sorry, pardon moi, for whatever anxiousness I may have caused you two. Do you forgive me, please?"

"Would you like coffee?" John asked then told her that we were the ones who should be asking for her forgiveness.

"Well, truth be told we waited for you to return to your room and at about 4 AM wanted to make sure our hotel passports worked."

Simone smiled and told us it was understandable and repeated how indebted she was for us joining her on this trip. She also shared with us some points from her meeting with Kiko the night before.

"We had a lovely dinner catching up on a lot of things. I haven't seen him in a long time. Of course, we talked about the Doctor and the tragedy, and the birth of Isabel. Kiko wanted to know a bit more about you and I told him the story about how you met my brother on St. John. He was intrigued that you took an interest and that lead to the present-day situation."

"Did he mention anything about the plan?

"Yes, we spoke about the objective of this trip which is, and that if all goes well, the opportunity to speak to Dr. Wu in person. That is why we are going to the museum today."

"Are we supposed to follow any specific directions?"

"Kiko said that everything was taken care of and that it would be best for you not to worry about all the details in advance. He assured me that all of that has been worked out personally by him."

"Okay, so we are going to the museum today?" I said finally joining into the conversation.

"Yes, I did question him about why the museum and he told me that that is where we will find Dr. Wu."

"His only direction was to remain casual and to pretend that we are interested in the exhibits on display there."

"That's a comfort," John said.

Simone then explained as much as she knew about the plan and we were on our way.

"We must be ready in one hour to leave for the Shanghai Museum. Kiko has arranged a special tour of the porcelain exhibit there. It is the largest collection in the world. Even the National Palace Museum in Taiwan does not have the comprehensive display of porcelain that dates to the Chung Dynasty. Once upon a time porcelain was worth more than land and gold," Simone said with genuine excitement in her voice then took her coffee and went to her suite to change.

John turned to me after she left us and said, "A porcelain exhibit? We came all this way to go to a museum?"

While I love a good museum, I must admit that he had a point. I told him we needed to trust Simone at this point.

"You know, John, there is a lot that we can learn from the largest collection of old pottery. Look at it this way, when handed clay, make a pot!" I finished my coffee and dove into the pool.

As we approached the doors to the lift, Simone asked John if he could access it. Once inside we laughed about the events the evening before and headed off for the Shanghai Museum.

Simone told us on the ride over that we would meet our guide at the Tea House located on the mezzanine level. We passed the main entrance to the museum and drove around the back to a discreet drive that led to an underground parking area. After our driver was checked in with security we were dropped off at the private entrance to the museum. Simone exited the Rolls first and we followed. Greeted by three additional security guards we were escorted to a private elevator. Once we arrived at the Tea House we were taken to a table and served green tea and Harvest Moon cakes, a Chinese pastry that is often filled with lotus seed paste or red bean and is traditionally served during the festival in mid-Autumn to celebrate the lunar moon. Given their popularity the museum serves them all year long.

After about fifteen minutes a tall man wearing a dark suit and horn rimmed glasses approached us. He spoke directly to Simone in French. Simone nodded to him and asked if we would like to see the porcelain exhibit she had talked about earlier that morning. I looked over at John and said,

"Of course, after all, that is why we are here!"

I smiled and then took the last bite of my Moon Cake.

At this point we were about to become active players in the plan that Kiko was about to direct. Simone playing the role of the leading lady, John and I, her stage hands.

We walked up a flight of stairs to the entrance of the exhibit. The man who had approached us earlier handed us three audio guides. We donned the apparatus and began our tour of the porcelain antiquities. Standing in front of the first display the audio tour began.

"Welcome to the Shanghai Museum. Here on exhibit you will find the oldest collection of porcelain in the world. Please follow the instructions provided, as it will make your time spent here ever so valuable. Remember to listen carefully and follow along with the instructions provided."

As we followed each of the numbered displays we learned more about the extensive history of porcelain. The guide informed us that porcelain was part of the evolution of the art of the potter. Its origins go back to about the same time as the development of agricultural techniques. In ancient China, pottery became essential not only for its purpose in everyday life, but also for ceremonial reasons as well. Pottery ownership became a measure of status and wealth as only the rich and powerful could afford funeral pottery. They contained life's necessities like water and rice that would be buried with the corpse.

I was learning that the oldest sources in China define porcelain as "fine compact pottery." The audio guide went on to explain that there is some debate regarding when Chinese porcelain was first made. There are four periods in Chinese history that have laid claims to its origin. I was so fascinated by the information I almost forgot about "the plan".

We were moving on from exhibit to exhibit when I noticed John's expression of concern. In front of exhibit number 32693 I understood why. The audio voice instructed us to switch to channel three on the audio devise. When I switched, it was a different voice. It was the voice of Kiko Foo according to the recording.

We had been instructed to remain casual as we continued the tour but to listen to the instructions carefully that he was about to give. He went on to say that Simone explained the night before that we are trusted friends and would be helpful in providing the needed decoy for the security guards assigned to the museum laboratory where Dr. Wu was working. He reminded us to be alert and adhere to the instructions provided. We were also told that we are being closely watched and again stressed that we follow his instructions.

"I want you to be assured that you will be able to leave China safely as long as you follow my instructions and remain interested in the porcelain collection on display. I've arranged a special tour of the museum's laboratory that is used in the study and restoration of porcelain." This was to be our next stop and Simone's opportunity to speak to Dr. Wu.

Kiko said that the audio guides would self-destruct at the end of the message. John and I quickly looked up, our eyes widened. Kiko then added, "I am joking; I've always wanted to say that, very Mission Impossible!"

Suddenly my audio device became muffled and I was unable to hear the rest of the message. Being in the "dark" about being in the dark became a great concern of mine. I looked over at John pretending to appreciate the pottery in the display case in front of us. I noticed that John was still taking in the information by the expression on his face. I gave him a bewildered look but his eye action told me to carry on. At this point of the tour an actual guide who said he would complete the tour and explain the rest of the articles on display met us.

"In this section, we are pleased to have in our collection some of the rarest porcelain in the world. The quality of each piece reflects the wealth of various dynasties. The rarity of porcelain is not just in the skill required to create it, but also the combination of ingredients. On display in this case is the finest example of crackle porcelain." It was then we learned about the discovery of mixing iron with the clay to create the most valuable of all porcelain pottery.

By adding iron to the clay at a temperature of 500 degrees Fahrenheit (an odd coincidence I thought), a chemical reaction occurs causing the iron to distribute within the clay base creating a crackly effect. This was considered the highest form of porcelain mastery. If the temperature rises too quickly or if the clay base contains any impurities, the result would not produce the fine lines within the porcelain. After hearing this, my mind wandered back to a story Samuel told us that required similar patience and precision.

Our guide announced that this portion of our arranged tour was over.

"Here at the Shanghai Museum, we hope that you now have a better understanding of the long and rich history of porcelain. Our collection represents that of the surviving pottery from the earliest times through the Tang Dynasty. The pieces in our exhibition constitute only a small part of the museum's collection but indeed represent each of the ancient periods."

Upon the conclusion of the tour the man who had handed us the audio devises appeared out of thin air and collected them back. In French, he said something to Simone, who then looked at us and then back to him. We were now being led by two security guards through a doorway that led to a staircase to take us to the basement of the museum. As we descended the stairs, John tried to whisper something to me that he heard on his audio recording that I did not. I tried to understand what he was whispering but the echo in the basement staircase made it impossible to hear what he was saying.

"This way please," said the taller of the two guards.

We were now turning left and descending a second staircase taking us three levels below the ground floor before we entered a poorly lit hallway. There we passed numerous vaults and were told that they housed the vast treasures of the museum. It may have been my imagination but to me they looked a bit like ancient crypts.

We reached the end of the hall where there was a security desk and two guards standing in front of a metal door. The security guard requested our passport. Simone turned to us, and with a smile asked if we would hand over our US passports for inspection. I looked at John and asked if he had our passports. John said no he left them at the hotel.

"I thought I heard you say you were getting them from the safe," I said.

"No, I thought you said you were getting them." He said with an unusual look on his face.

"No, you were the last one in the room, remember?" I snipped.

I was certain about two things at this point. First, John did say he would get our passports and, second, he was the last one in the room. I quickly thought that there must be a reason he denied both facts. Maybe it had something to do with what he tried to explain to me on the staircase.

"I am so sorry but we don't have them," John said to Simone.

The security guard at the desk spoke to Simone.

"They can't enter the laboratory Madame."

"Pardon moi?"

"Pardon moi?" the security guard repeated in a mocking tone.

"It is the Chinese government's rule that no one enters restricted areas without having their passports recorded!"

We were told to go back to the hotel and retrieve our passports to register at this security point. It was protocol, otherwise our noncompliance would be reported to the local authorities.

One of the security guards then said to Simone,

"You should stay here. If you decide to go back with them the meeting that you came for may not take place. I don't think it can be rearranged so quickly should there be any further delay. Consider that the future may not be so generous upon your return."

When he told her that I thought I saw him wink at her, however under the circumstances, aka stress, I may have been imagining it.

Simone graciously then said, "But, of course. They can go back to the hotel and get them and then join us back here at the security desk as you instruct, oui?"

The guard nodded.

We could tell that the security guard speaking was the higher ranking of the three by the number of stars pinned across his uniform. As the one in command, the other two guards followed his instructions. We turned without saying a word and began walking back down the long hallway with the locked vaults. We were taken to the underground exit of the museum. Simone remained behind with the senior guard who had given the instructions.

John and I were being escorted back to our hotel by two security guards to collect our passports. I was still a bit confused about the situation given what John said earlier about having retrieved them from the safe in our hotel room.

When we arrived at the hotel we headed for the elevator while the driver along with the two escorts waited in the lobby.

"What is going on?" I said to John.

"I don't have time to explain everything, I need to use your computer. Trust me everything is going to be fine."

I wanted to believe that everything would be fine so I didn't bother him with more questions. Once we got to the penthouse floor he went directly over to my computer. I just stood nearby in case he needed me to help. While I was standing behind him all I could think about was the beach vacation that we'd given up to be here.

"Hand me my cell phone, please."

I went over to the sofa where he left his jacket and felt around the pockets to find his phone along with our passports! Now I was really confused, why did he say he didn't have them back at the museum?

"Hello, look what I found."

"Hand me my phone and I'll explain it later."

This was the second time I was told an explanation was forthcoming. I was not so sure about the situation, just like I wasn't too sure about "the plan" surrounding this entire ordeal. I handed him his phone while I held our passports tightly in my other hand. He took his phone and began dialing.

"We need to secure our departure out of China and I was told by Kiko on the audio guide tape to call this number as soon as we got back to our hotel.

I realized at that moment this must have been what I missed on the recording when my audio became fuzzy.

"Hello yes. I've entered the site you provided. This is it... yes I see it on the screen," said John into the phone.

"OK, the code is 040893... OK, I entered it."

John then told me to hand him his passport.

I watched him open his passport and place it over the screen. He then started to enter another code into the computer as per the instructions he received over the phone. Upon hitting the last digit, the screen turned from blue to an intense orange.

"Now give me yours."

He repeated the same sequence of keys on the computer keyboard as I watched the screen change to orange.

"Thanks, I think we are done," he said into the phone.

"Okay now that's done we need to get back to the museum."

"Right," I said.

I followed him out to the elevator and after entering the passcode we descended to the lobby in complete silence. I knew better than to ask him what was going on in front of the guards waiting for us in the lobby area. Our entourage was waiting in the same spot where we had left them. Judging from the cigarette butts in the ashtray it looked like each guard went through a pack of cigarettes. They seemed anxious to get us back to the museum.

"We are all set," John said when we approached them. He held our passports up to assure them we had them. I continued to follow John as we left the hotel. The five of us walked towards the car without saying a word.

Within minutes we were back on the road heading to the museum. This time the car pulled behind the building and we entered the laboratory from a differ passageway. We quickly reached the security check point in the belly of the museum following our escorts.

"Did you get your passports?" The senior guard asked. "Fine. I'll take them and make photo copies for the record. You can wait here until Madame Oppenheimer is finished."

Within minutes Simone appeared.

"I am so very sorry that you had to drive back, I hope that you were not too inconvenienced. I am all done here so your timing is perfect."

As we walked the long hallway out to the underground garage, Simone asked us if we noticed how bright the sun seems to glow when one exits a dark room. John agreed and smiled saying, "Especially when one walks into the orange sunlight!" John smiled at Simone who smiled back at us as we pulled out into the light. It wasn't the black Rolls that had brought us back to the museum but a Bentley with a different driver. I noticed it was the senior security guard who had just greeted us with our passports. He was driving us in the opposite direction of our hotel. I asked Simone and John if this was also part of the plan. The driver's divider window now lowered and a passenger in the front seat spoke.

"Simone, I hope you learned what you needed to learn."

"I did, thank you." Simone replied. The man then said, "Now Simone, you have exactly two hours to clear customs and board for your return to Paris. Gentlemen, you will be boarding a separate flight direct to New York."

I thought to myself how crazy it was to spend less than 48 hours in China. Simone then told us she wanted to introduce us to Kiko before our departure. I assumed that she meant at the airport.

"Kiko, I would like you to meet my traveling companions."

At the same time, John and I repeated the name.

"Kiko!"

Kiko then turned around to face us and smiled.

I then asked Kiko if what we just did was the plan?

"Yes, it was and you all did an excellent job."

"Good, I think I will celebrate with a drink when I get to the airport!"

"What are you thinking of having?"

"On a day like today, Grey Goose up with one olive."

There was universal agreement on my choice as we pulled up to our first stop. As Simone exited the car she reassured us that we were in good hands.

"Kiko will make sure all goes well. Thank you so much and we will talk soon. I promise you that!" She leaned over to give us both a kiss on the check and was out of the car heading into the terminal. When she was out of sight, the car moved on.

"Kiko, what about our belongings at the hotel?"

"Not to worry, they have already been sent for and will be on your flight, along with a token of appreciation from Simone."

The car pulled up to the American Airlines terminal and stopped. Kiko handed us an envelope and wished us a safe flight. We got out and started to walk towards the door when we heard Kiko from the car shout, “Bon Voyage!”

“What the…? What is—oh I only hope we are flying back first-class after all of this.” John looked at me then took a deep breath.

We headed towards the customs desk where John went first. After he passed through and it was my turn. I handed over my passport. The official inside the glass booth looked down at my photo then up to me. I smiled, he did not. When he laid my passport over his security device I noticed from outside the booth the screen inside turned from blue to orange just as it did on my computer back at the hotel only hours earlier. He looked up at me and this time he smiled. I held my breath and tried to look calm. He then nodded and handed me back my passport.

“Have a nice flight,” he said as I took my passport from him and began to walk away. When I looked up I saw that John was waiting nearby. What I didn’t expect is that he was standing next to an armed soldier. For a second I thought of possibly walking past them until John smiled and said, “We’re over here”.

The soldier escorted us to a hallway where hidden from the public space was a doorway leading to another check point.

"This way," he said, and without hesitating we followed.

We passed this new checkpoint location when another soldier greeted us. With one soldier in the front of us and two behind us we started to walk towards an exit door that led to the tarmac where there was a private jet getting ready for takeoff. The second soldier turned and in perfect English told us to have a nice day.

We entered the salon and a flight attendant took the envelope from John and showed us to our seats, of which there were only 4. On two of the seats there were large Louis Vuitton duffel bags.

"Those are for you, they have your belongings from the hotel, computer included, plus a little something extra." The attendant turned and within minutes returned to our seats and handed us two Grey Goose martinis with one olive and said, "I heard you might need one."

After takeoff John suggested we look in our bags to see what the "something extra" was. Before I even agreed he had already unzipped the bag to discover a tin of Beluga caviar. Along with the caviar was a sterling silver container filled with toast points. I opened mine to discover a leather box containing a Faberge letter opener. In both bags, Simone had placed a miniature lead soldier wearing a Black Watch plaid kilt and a note, "A soldier from the Highlands in Scotland known for protecting the land and its inhabitants. Thank you. Love Simone."

I held it in my hand and though this was a rather strange trip. I was happy that we did it but happier that we were going home. We toasted Simone and our short adventure and quickly fell into a deep sleep as we passed between the earth and the stars along the way.

On our terrace, a few days later we opened a bottle of champagne to celebrate our safe return. It was then that John explained that the orange code at the airport provided diplomatic clearance allowing global travel to any destination without restrictions.

"But why did we have to leave the museum to do it?" I asked.

"It was all part of the plan. We provided a distraction so that Simone had time to talk to Dr. Wu without all the guards being nearby. The best part of this whole ordeal is we have that diplomatic status anywhere in the world. It's like an E-Z pass for swanky international jet-set people like us. Even if we were carrying the Dowager's finest Mother of Pearl salad server, we would not have been stopped from leaving China."

We ended our night falling asleep outside on the terrace chairs. Sleeping next to the Hudson River, we were far away from the Huanpuwe River in China. I got up at a certain point to cover John with his favorite flannel orange blanket, pashmina for the masses, and walked to look over the railing at the river. It was relatively quiet for New York on a Sunday. In the distance, you could hear crickets chirping. They say in China the sound of a cricket means that good fortune is near.

Chapter Seventeen

"The House Call"

After we returned to New York we went back to our daily routine. We didn't bother taking the rest of our two-week break and ended up going back into the office. On Wednesday evening, we were about ready to sit down with our cocktails when I asked John if he had checked the mail as I poured two glasses of Cabernet.

"Not yet," he said as he was pouring some cashews into the silver container that previously held toast points Simone gave us as well as a tin of Beluga. I told him that I would meet him on the patio as I handed over a bowl of olives telling him that was our dinner and laughed.

John went out to the patio and I stayed behind to open the mail, mostly junk, until I discovered the envelope with the powder blue crown signet of Columbia University on the return side. I could tell that it was hand delivered because our doorman had signed for it. I reached for the martini shaker thinking that I would rather have something stronger so, leaving my glass of red wine to the side, I mixed a cold one before I left the kitchen to open the letter.

John was still on the terrace arranging cushions and lighting the candles when I sat in front of the fireplace and reached for the elegant letter opener Simone gave us. Before I opened it, I took a long sip of my drink. For a moment, I admired the red and gold enamel handle of the Faberge letter opener and as I inserted the tip into the envelopes I noticed the gold cabochon on the handle was loose.

John called out, “Hurry! The sun is setting and it is the most intense red and orange that I have seen yet.” I placed the letter opener down on the coffee table and called out that I would be there in a minute. Thinking to myself was it as intense as code orange on a computer screen? I took the letter out to the terrace and read it to John.

Dear Sirs,

This is the most secure way to connect with you. I needed to insure receipt of this note with confidence. It would be best if I made a house call to your home, this evening preferably.

Sincerely,

Dr. Williams
Chair, Atomic Development, Columbia University

As if we were in a Wes Anderson movie the doorbell rang within seconds of reading the note. I handed him the note and took a sip of my drink and went to see who was at the door.

"Good evening, I am Dr. Williams. I hope I am not intruding." I told him we just read his note but we were not expecting to see him so soon.

"My apologies. I didn't want to allow too much time to go by before seeing you."

John invited him into the apartment.

"I'll make this very quick. You see my visit is for your own safety. This matter takes on a sense of urgency and I would like to be helpful," he said as he entered the apartment.

"But of course, please make yourself comfortable." I took a sip of my drink.

"I hope that you are not alarmed by this sudden visit. You have nothing to fear. I am just here to ask a few questions about your trip to Shanghai."

John and I looked at each other and while trying to disguise my anxiety I offered him a glass of wine to ease my nerves.

"Thank you, that would be very nice."

"Go ahead out to the terrace and I will be right out."

John led the doctor outside. I turned and went into the kitchen and took the untouched glass that I had poured earlier. When I stepped outside the two were standing by the railing looking over the Hudson River. They were talking about the congested river front across the way on the Jersey side.

"Overbuilt piles of condominiums stacked one on top of the another." He told us that he had a similar river view from his bedroom and he felt like all the development happened overnight. I thought the topic of condominium expansion on the river would never end until John suggested that we take a seat to talk.

It quickly became clear to both of us that Dr. Williams knew quite a bit about our travel to China. In fact, we learned that he had been following our moves since our first visit to Columbia's library. It was the two-forged library passes that tipped him off, at least that is what he told us.

"I had been informed by campus security that there were two men asking a lot of questions pertaining to what we consider sensitive data. That raised a red flag for us.

"Us?" I said.

"It isn't unusual for students and professors to be inquiring into the work of Dr. Oppenheimer. What is a red flag, so to speak, is the interest you have in the work that he did with Dr. Wu. That work is highly classified and anyone doing any investigation into it without proper clearance is considered a concern to certain people that I am not at liberty to mention."

I now thought that our code orange wasn't going to get us out of this one.

"I was notified by campus security after the third computer request. I told them not to question you thinking that there might be something more to your interest in Oppenheimer. My instinct was validated when I got a call a month ago from Simone Oppenheimer. You know her, correct?"

At this point, John suggested that perhaps we end our conversation until we had time to contact our lawyer.

"That's not necessary." The doctor said. "You aren't in any trouble with the law, at least not yet."

"Not yet?" I said.

"If we are not in any trouble why are you here?" John asked.

"Honestly this has more to do with the CIA, than me."

"Oh, that must be the 'us', correct?'

"Yes. That's right. They are interested in understanding what your relationship is to Madame Oppenheimer."

He was never very specific about any of the details to the point that I wondered if he was telling us the truth. He took a sip of his wine then began to explain more.

"The CIA considers the work that Dr. Oppenheimer and Dr. Wu did at the University to be highly classified. They were contacted by officials that individuals without security clearance were inquiring about it, that's what triggered their concern."

I asked what were they concerned about?

"The research that Dr. Wu and Dr. Oppenheimer were working on was confidential. It was a project that was partly funded by the U.S. Government. It was so top-secret that only a handful of people at Columbia were aware of it. I don't even think the former Chair of the department was in the know." The exchange taking place between the doctor and us was becoming a bit more relaxed until he got to this point in his conversation.

"The CIA continues to be interested in Dr. Wu, even more so after I got the call from Simone Oppenheimer. It appears that the government would like to find out what Dr. Wu is working on. They know that I am here talking with you. If you look down and across to the statue of Franz Sigel at the entrance to Riverside Park, you will see that they are watching."

John and I walked out to the terrace to peek over the railing and we noticed a large black van at the end of the block. Dr. Williams then asked if he could have a second glass of wine

"How well do you know Madame Oppenheimer?"

"Not that well. We met her in Paris a few months ago at a restaurant."

"Did you know that she was married to the scientist Oppenheimer?"

"Why do you ask? And what business…"

John interrupted me.

"What does that have to do with anything?"

"A great deal," said the Doctor.

"You see, this is what it comes down to, everyone wants to get their hands on the same information. The fact that this case has been dormant for so long is a good indication that no one is leading in the discovery of something that can make billions of dollars. The CIA traced the disappearance of Dr. Wu back to the Chinese government long ago. Even though no one has seen him, that is until recently, and the CIA knows who that is."

"We don't know who that is."

"The CIA thinks otherwise."

"Well, they are wrong." I said. "And if they thought otherwise why weren't they speaking to us directly instead of you, unless you're working for them." This remark did not go over very well. John was not too pleased with my outburst either and spoke.

"So, tell us Dr. Williams, what do we have to do in all of this? We only traveled to Shanghai as guests of Simone to see the porcelain exhibit at the museum."

"We know about your visit and the security check, not to mention the clever plan to return to the hotel to retrieve your passports."

"I'm not sure what you're talking about."

"You most certainly do. The Chinese government now knows that one of the security guards was part of the entire farce and that Dr. Wu had an unexpected visitor. The CIA now knows where Dr. Wu is as well. Whomever it was that planned your entrance to and from the Shanghai Museum has the authorities, both Chinese and American, let's say, rather concerned."

John, placing his glass on the table next to the letter opener, repeated my earlier question in a more diplomatic tone.

"If both governments are so concerned about this why did the CIA send you to question us?" Dr. Williams smiled then sipped his wine.

"The U.S. government realizes that this is a very delicate situation and is trying to avoid unnecessary publicity. They also know that you did nothing illegal in your actions and so to minimize any potential issues they have asked me to be the messenger, an emissary, so to speak, of the U.S. government." The Doctor took another sip.

"Is that why we are being watched from below?" It was apparent that after John's question the Doctor was becoming a bit agitated.

"I am instructed to tell you that the government hopes that you can help them with whatever information you may have or more importantly, can find out from Simone Oppenheimer." I then interrupted Dr. Williams.

"You haven't answered the question! Why are we being watched?"

"You are not being watched, just protected."

"From whom?"

The Doctor only smiled.

After a long pause, he finished his wine and robotically repeated that the purpose of his visit was to inform us that we were expected to cooperate with the CIA and provide any information about Simone and her meeting at the museum.

"You must from this moment on report any contact with Madame Oppenheimer and inform the officials through me. Also, I'd suggest you forego any plans to travel any time soon."

He then handed us a card with his personal number instructing us to call him if we heard from Simone. Just before he left the apartment he turned and said,

"You don't happen to know who arranged the guided museum tour for you in Shanghai?"

Chapter Eighteen

"Missing You"

What were we getting ourselves into? An innocent inquiry about an abandoned beach house was turning into a James Patterson novel. There was little comfort knowing that we were under the protection of the CIA which we suspected Dr. Williams was in cahoots with after seeing him get into the black van parked on the corner. John signaled in a rather creative form of sign language for us not to speak. His pantomime suggested that our apartment may be bugged. Thinking that he was probably right I went into the bedroom to get two pads and pens. While I was doing that he put a Nancy Lamont CD on just in case one of us slipped.

He handed me his pad with a message.

I don't like this situation at all. Why would the CIA be asking about Simone when it is obvious that they already know she is living in Paris? Am I missing something? I'm also not happy about us being told we can't leave the country, seems a bit dramatic, no? What did he mean by 'forego any travel'? I'm not sure about what is going on, what about you?

I looked at John and nodded my head in agreement. At the same time, I picked up the Faberge letter opener to tighten the gold cap. Turning it clockwise the cap came off the handle. I realized at that moment that it was meant to be tightened counter clockwise. John watched as the cap fell to the floor. Bending over to retrieve the it, a note that had been rolled up and inserted into the handle, fell out. I looked up at John.

"Would you like another drink?"

"Yes. That would be nice, thank you."

John moved to the sofa where I was seated as I unfurled the note.

Gentlemen,

I am hopeful that you have discovered this note. Do not be alarmed but be cautious with who you speak to as it pertains to your recent trip. We were concerned about security which is why we have provided you with follow up instructions in this manner. We knew that you and Simone were being trailed from the moment you arrived in China.

This explains why we wanted you to leave the country right after your visit to the museum. I realize that you may have thought the "plan" ended with your return home, but we need you to help Simone again. Unfortunately, there is a great deal at stake and we are requesting your continued service and apologize for the very short notice. What you must know is that Simone learned something vital to help a lot of people while in the company of Dr. Wu. She will I'm sure explain it all to you when you meet.

While this all may seem cryptic, what I am asking of you is to meet Simone on St. John as soon as you can. She too is being watched but we have arranged a way to get her there without being noticed. Your next move is to call this number at any public phone and provide the password, Moon Cakes.

Looking forward to thanking you in person and soon.

Sincerely,
Kiko

We looked at each other in silence. Knowing that we needed to find a place where we could talk John suggested that we get something to eat.

"Let's go out a grab a bite to eat. We can decide where once we are out."

I agreed and we took off.

We talked along the way but were cautious assuming we were being followed. When we got to our favorite Indian restaurant John went to the back where he knew there was a pay phone, one of the very few left in the NYC. He called the number provide and when it was answered he said.

"Moon Cakes."

"Moon Cakes." The voice repeated then proceeded to give him instructions.

The first step was to call Samuel and tell him how much we missed him and the island. Of course, he told John how much he missed us, most of all our 4 o'clock cocktail. From the earlier instructions from Kiko that meant we should arrive at the ferry dock on St. John at 4 PM. We later learned that Samuel would be working on the other end letting Judy know we were on our way, no questions asked. The second step was leave the next day as we would normally do for work. After the call, John joined me at the table and we ordered Butter Chicken, Tikka Masala and a side of garlic Nan.

With the assumption that we were being watched we left our apartment building that morning and headed to Grand Central Terminal as instructed the evening before. We knew the morning rush hour congestion would work in our favor if we were being trailed. The plan was to take a detour into the Oyster Bar for breakfast. It was the perfect place to lose someone if one was being followed. The location of the restaurant is below street level and can be accessed from multiple entrances from within Grand Central. Inside the restaurant there are a series of arches constructed resembling ancient catacombs. The place spans almost a block long in length and the expansive space is divided into three sections. The center bar with a counter and many stools, the main dining room, and a separate pub like room that is unknown by most tourists. We had been there before but were unaware of the back door that led to an underground passage connecting to the subway (I imagine that makes it convenient for a secret rendezvous as well).

We finished our coffee and asked for the check. Just as Moon Cakes said, the airline tickets were in the billfold presented with the check along with directions to exit by way of the back door. Off we went and down into the subway station hoping that we could get away unseen. We had never taken the express "train to the plane" that the city has tried desperately to get going but it was only steps from the No. 4 subway line. We got to the airport making a note that the "train to the plane" did have great merit. We departed for St. Thomas on the 10 AM flight which ensured that we would make the ferry to St. John on time. Upon our departure, we both realized that there was no passport check to leave the US for St. John but not knowing where we would wind up this time we would have to hope our diplomatic status for travel was for real.

We traveled from the airport in St. Thomas and waited in the back of the Green Parrot bar opposite the ferry dock for St. John. We hoped that we were not being followed and knew we would be missed when we didn't show up at home that night. It would take a few days for them to figure out where we were, and the one thing I knew, is that they would. While in the past, margaritas were required as we waited for the ferry, this time we did without. We sat quietly waiting, me with a copy of People and John wearing oversized Jackie O sunglasses.

Anyway…

Chapter Nineteen

"Deep Water"

Making it from New York to St. John is what they call in the game of chess a King's Gambit, one of the oldest opening moves only played by experts. We managed to leave the city without being stopped or followed. Like the player who chooses to employ the King's Gambit in their first move leaving their King exposed, we too risked being captured.

Judy was waiting at the dock in Cruz Bay as our ferry pulled in. She told us that everything was set for us for our stay at Kokomo Cottage. She even laughed about telling the renters who had booked the place at the same time as our unexpected arrival, that they must have gotten the wrong brochure then moved them to a friend's house down the road. She also knew that there was only so much we could tell her about the topic of the iron gate but knew that is what something important that we had gotten ourselves into. On the way to the cottage Judy mentioned that Miss Lucy's restaurant was suddenly closed.

"Miss Lucy never closes her restaurant. She is open 7 days a week 12 months of the year. Even when we are in the thick of a storm, she always has something cooking on the stove."

"That's odd. Did Samuel tell you where she went?"

"Yes, he mentioned that she and Isabel were over on St. Thomas and didn't have much more to say about it. He told me that when he asked if I could meet you at the 4 o'clock ferry. He said that you should meet him tomorrow around 6 down at Ship Wreck."

"Thanks, how about tonight, will you stick around a while and have a few drinks?"

"Sounds good, I may even spend the night on the veranda if that's okay with you."

"Are you kidding? You're always welcome to stay at your own house, especially after we arrived with little advanced notice."

"No kidding. The renters didn't have a clue about what was going on. That's funny, right?

"Well, I am sure you will make it up to them

somehow."

"Already have. They have a free dinner at Shipwreck!"

"Oh, how generous of you."

We all stared to laugh and once we settled on the veranda and had a few martini's, I was then comforted by the ever-present Virgin Gorda in the moonlight.

The next morning, we were chilling at the cottage as best we could. Starting out with coffee we couldn't wait to see Samuel and listen to what he had to say. He would know when Simone would be arriving on the island. I couldn't help but wonder about Dr. Williams back in New York and how soon he and his CIA buddies would figure out where we were. I was certain that they knew we had taken off.

In the small parking area next to Shipwreck, Samuel was standing waiting for our arrival. After greeting us we headed inside the restaurant where Judy took a seat at the bar and we three sat at the same back table we occupied a few months earlier. The energy in the place seemed good, comforting and protective. We ordered a few drinks and after they were served Samuel began to fill us in on why we were all there. Just as I expected he too had gotten all his instructions from Kiko.

"I was lucky to get the call when Kiko phoned. My sister Lucy was out buying fish for her restaurant and I was there to answer the phone."

"What did he tell you?"

"Kiko, what kind of name is that?"

"It's short for Kikkoman, a traditional Japanese name which means spicy one."

"How do you know that?"

"I looked it up."

Then John turned back to Samuel and asked what Kiko said to him.

"He said that he was waiting to hear from you before putting the plan into motion."

"Oh no, another plan, what's the plan?" John flashed me a look and told Samuel to continue.

"The first thing he told me was that Simone had to be very careful. She was being watched and could be in danger. The trip to China ended up creating a lot of attention and there are people out there who are not happy about it."

"What people?"

"He didn't go into specific about who they were but said that Simone needed to travel to the island to get something. Again, he was very vague about what it was but assured me that it was of the utmost importance."

"Are you telling us that Simone is here?"

"Yes. She's over on Virgin Gorda. The plan is for us to meet her tomorrow at the beach house."

"What about Isabel and Miss Lucy?" Samuel told us that Lucy was aware of something going on after she talked to her cousin.

"My cousin had gotten a call from Simone asking about Lucy and Isabel just a few days ago. She also told her that she was planning a short trip to St. John. Simone knew that our cousin would call Lucy to tell her as soon as they hung up. She also knew that the information would be enough to make Lucy take Isabel to St. Thomas for a visit with my cousin. I think my sister Lucy thought that

Simone was returning to St. John to take Isabel back to Paris. She doesn't want anything to do with Simone."

I smiled at John and was thinking that something wasn't making any sense.

"Why would Simone contact a cousin that she hadn't seen or spoken to in years unless there was a reason and was that reason to get Isabel and Lucy off the island?"

"I think she wanted Lucy off the island and out of her way when she got here. It might have something to do with what she came back to collect, and it's not Isabel. Not this time at least."

Samuel then laughed and ordered us a second round of drinks. Other than letting us know about the information obtained from Kiko and his assumptions about Miss Lucy he told us how happy he was to see us and how happy he was to be reconnected to Simone. Then he mentioned something that Simone said that he thought was important and that we should know.

"After Simone got back from China she told me that something clicked in her head about the experiment that the

Doctor was last working on."

"The same experiment that Dr. Wu was working on too?"

"Yes. I think so."

John told him that during the visit by Dr. Williams we were told that the CIA was interested in the same thing.

"The man kept asking us questions about our trip to China with Simone." Samuel took a sip from his Red Stripe beer. Putting it down he said,

"I am so very grateful and while I do not know all that there is going on here, I do know that Simone was so pleased that you were there for her then and here for her now."

John raised his glass and announced, "A toast. Who would have thought that our snooping around a short time ago would lead us here? To Simone!"

So there the three of us sat talking about everything that happened and how little we all really knew. I found it interesting that Simone mentioned to Samuel that she needed to find something on the island that was an important part of the plan. What Samuel was most excited about was seeing Simone after so many years.

"It's a wish come true, a wish come true."

We joined Judy at the bar where she was socializing with a few friends. After one more drink she asked if we were ready to leave. We said our goodnight to Samuel, Ellie, and, of course, the pirates wishing them a peaceful rest. Judy got us back safely, avoiding the goats on the side of the road.

The next day Samuel walked down to the cottage and quickly got us up. We dressed and the three of us headed up the road where his Jeep was still running. When we got down to the beach we saw a woman standing on the shore wearing white and gently waving. She smiled and said: "The Doctor once told me you never have to fear deep water as long as someone you trust is watching you from the shore."

Chapter Twenty

"Just A Pinch"

We walked with Simone around to the back of the house where she told us more about her meeting with Dr. Wu. She wanted us to know that she learned back in Shanghai how valuable the work was that he and the Doctor had been doing at the university.

"Their work could possibly be the salvation for millions of people. Dr. Wu told me it was for humanitarian reasons, and not for the sake of profit. Dr. Wu discovered that they were being watched while they were conducting experiments. He told me that it wasn't until he was kidnapped by his own country that the American government inquired about the work and motive behind his disappearance. Wu said the Chinese suspected that this discovery could potentially lead to enormous profits. He told me that they were his kidnappers and the Doctor had nothing to do with it which is what the authorities suspected at the time. The CIA thought otherwise, which is what led to the Doctor's dismissal from Columbia University. It was the end of their collaboration."

As we sat in the garden out back, Simone pointed out the spot where Samuel had discovered the Doctor after his fall.

"I haven't been back here since that night. Even time hasn't erased the pain that I feel when I think about it. Fallen and left behind. I think about the Doctor all the time and maybe it's good that I am back here, another step towards the process of healing I suppose. I feel his presence."

The area where he had died was now covered over by vegetation. Breaking our momentary silence was Samuel who walked up with refreshments that he had stored in the back of his Jeep. He obviously had anticipated this moment and presented the bottles of Rose wine and a tray of cheese. Simone stood up and began to hug him, it was a reunion of family. John and I decided to take a walk on the beach. We thought it was the right thing to give them some time alone. After a few minutes, we looked back to see them laughing as if time and circumstances had never separated them. Eventually, they began to walk towards the beach hand in hand.

"I never thought this day would come," Samuel said as they caught up to us.

"Being together with Simone back here at the house, I just never thought it would happen."

When we returned to the house Samuel opened the bottle of wine and poured us all a glass. He raised his glass and said with tears in his eyes:

"No, I never thought this day would come and here we are. Welcome home!"

He wiped a tear from his ebony cheek. Simone then stood up and held her glass with her toast.

"To my husband, and my family including the newest members."

Simone looked over at us as did Samuel.

We sat for a moment silent, until Simone said we didn't have a great deal of time and she needed a moment to explain what had to be done. But before she continued, she asked Samuel about Isabel. “Are they together on St. Thomas?”

“Yes,” he replied with a grin. “She is away on St. Thomas and sister Lucy thinks that you are looking for her.

“Good,” said Simone. “Our cousin did get my message to Lucy in time. You may not completely understand what this is all about yet. Let me explain.

We sat until late afternoon without questioning anything that Simone had planned.

“Samuel, do you remember when the Doctor wanted me to mix the foam that would come from his boiling of the salt water? He insisted that I wait until the water temperature reached five hundred degrees Fahrenheit then add a pinch. Remember that?”

“Yes, I remember,” Samuel smiled. “Well, it seems that that is the essential requirement for the formula to take on other properties.”

Simone said that she only remembered that after her meeting with Dr. Wu at the Shanghai Museum. It was something he said about her husband that stuck in her mind for days after seeing him. Dr. Wu reminded her how meticulous her husband was in the laboratory. That statement triggered something deep in her memory. It was the time that her husband told her in the kitchen what the essential element was to successfully create the foam. In her mind, she still could hear him say, "This is the final ingredient to cause the reaction needed for the salt water and the foam to overflow".

"Of course, he had told you just a pinch." Samuel said remembering the time in the kitchen.

"When I had the conversation with Dr. Wu, he told me that he was still working on some of the research that he and the Doctor were conducting. It was no longer his passion but he was being forced to do it by the Chinese government. He mentioned that without his notes he couldn't remember the sequence of adding a certain element to complete the experiment. Dr. Wu was very frail when I saw him, perhaps as the result of the pressure he was under doing his work for his government. While I was there he tried to get a beaker of salt water at 500 degrees

Fahrenheit to create a top layer of foam. It reminded me of something but I couldn't put my finger on it. Unfortunately, Dr. Wu had no success. He said that he couldn't remember what it was that would trigger the reaction." When I looked over to Samuel he had a wide grin on his face as if he knew where the story was going. Simone took a sip of her wine then continued speaking.

"I told Dr. Wu that I wished I could be of help but at the time I did not know how I could. I left the laboratory feeling that there was something strangely familiar about his question. As the three of us then reunited at the security desk and began to walk towards the underground exit I heard in my heart the Doctor's voice reminding me, as he did so many times right here at the house, what was needed to complete the process."

"So, what was it?" I said.

Simone told us that it was weeks later when she was back in Paris that it came to her.

"I was in the kitchen making a late-night snack and when I reached for the salt I heard his voice in my head.

He said, 'Simone you must feel the grains in your hand and then you will know the proper amount to add. Just a pinch that is all it will take, you'll see.' That was it. That is what Dr. Wu couldn't remember about the experiment." We sat there at the concrete table delighted that she was convinced that she was on to something. What John and I did understand is that our trip to Shanghai had provided the information that Simone needed to begin to make it right. Simone told us that she needed us to do one more thing before we departed.

"Of course, but where to now?" John said with a mischievous grin.

"Tonight, I will tell you that part of our agenda, but, for now you must trust me once more and return to Kokomo. I will meet you around 9 o'clock at Miss Lucy's. There is something there that I know is of great importance."

It was dark when Samuel dropped us off at the driveway leading down to the cottage. After a few glasses of wine earlier he didn't want to risk navigating down the drive. We didn't relish the prospect of becoming unwelcome guests for the goats below.

Chapter Twenty-One

"Vanity Fair "

Someone was waiting for us down by the cottage when we got back from the beach. We heard a sound ahead by an abandoned wooden hut. Stopping in our tracks, we listened closely. It was very dark as clouds were passing in front of the moon obstructing her beams from shining down. We stepped back to make sure we were not in eyesight from the cottage. Sounds again came from the wooden hut halfway down to the cottage. A baby goat rambled down the steep side of the cliff adjacent to the drive. The muffled sound became clear as we got closer and that's when we stopped in our tracks. It was Judy hiding in the hut calling out to warn us not to go down the rest of the way to Kokomo. I wasn't sure which was more alarming the innocent baby goat coming out of nowhere or the owl-like sound coming from Judy.

We waited until it got darker, and then began climbing up to the road. Judy was smart enough to park her truck in a driveway opposite the entrance to Kokomo. Once we were all aboard, she drove us down to the Shipwreck Inn where we were to wait for Simone to call her. Seems the CIA contacted the local police on the island asking questions about us. Judy overheard the conversation in front of Dave's Pirate Scuba Bar directly across from the Shipwreck Inn. She knew by the description the CIA provided, that they were looking for us. Only two days on the island and they had already tracked us down.

Judy thought that the Shipwreck Inn would be the safest place to go because we had friends there. Friends on the island don't talk, especially to the CIA. Ellie saw us from the bar and told us to take a table in the back.

"Are you hungry?"

I looked over at the counter and spotted a Key Lime pie under a plastic dome.

"How about a slice of that pie and two forks, please."

"Coming right over."

Behind me on a shelf was a pile of magazines mostly left behind by tourists. I picked up an old copy of

Vanity Fair magazine that was on top. I began flipping through the magazine when I discovered an article about Blue Water International. It mentioned a French company and its monopoly on water filtration plants in China. With the growing problem of a polluted water supply, drinkable water was becoming expensive to provide. As a result, the government of China was working on a solution that would eliminate the dependency on the French company. Thus Dr. Wu and his work in the laboratory at the museum.

Judy and John decided to play pool to ease their nerves as Ellie brought us over some coffee. I declined their invitation to join in as I was too engrossed in the Vanity Fair article that was a year old. I learned that Blue Water was at the time operating in twenty-five cities throughout China and planning expansions into another twenty within two years. The journalist stated that the expansion was solely for profit, not altruistic purposes. If you couldn't afford to pay the price for their service, your water spigot would be removed and you would then have to rely on the polluted river that negligent companies, including Blue Water International, had created. It was estimated that one out of every three people in China would not have access to clean water.

I showed John the article when he returned to our table. Scanning it quickly he turned to me and said, "Now I understand what we are doing here."

"Me too." I replied.

I closed the magazine and took a sip of coffee.

Judy's phone rang and without answering she suggested that we retreat to the back of the bar. Walking out the back door of the Shipwreck Inn Judy passed us the keys to her truck and told us to drive down to Miss Lucy's. She said that she would be by later to get it back. As we pulled out we noticed that Ellie was out on the patio talking to the police. She must have seen us from the corner of her eye because as we passed she made a sweeping gesture with her right hand pointing in the opposite direction that we were heading.

Chapter Twenty-Two

"Tin Boxes"

We drove Judy's truck to Miss Lucy's as instructed. The first thing we noticed when we pulled into the driveway of Miss Lucy's was a hand written closed sign on the front door and a dim light on inside the kitchen. John and I walked around the back. We saw Simone and Samuel in the kitchen. Simone was searching through the numerous recipe boxes on the shelf over the sink, while Samuel stood silently leaning on the cold stove watching her. It was obvious to us that she was looking for something. We entered from the back door.

"What are you looking for?" I asked.

Simone looked up for a second and said in a low whisper "something that is very important." I thought she said something about a recipe box. We walked over to Samuel and like him just watched Simone in action.

John then asked Samuel if he thought we could be of any help.

"I already asked and she told me to just stand still and be quiet," said Samuel.

The three of us did just that. After a few minutes, I walked into the dining room area to check if we had been followed. The street was pitch black and the only sound filtering though the darkness was the occasional cackle of the chickens in the front yard of the restaurant. Returning to the kitchen the three occupants hadn't moved from their positions.

"Where did she put it? What did she do with it? Where is it?"

We just stood silently by as Simone continued to search the kitchen. Drawer after drawer, shelf after shelf, whatever it was she was searching for seemed to be of the utmost importance.

"Can we help?", asked John again. This only intensified her search until she finally looked back up at us and said, "Sorry boys, I really need to find something I placed in a tin box a long time ago. It was a recipe box that belonged to my mother. I couldn't find it back at the beach house so I assumed that Lucy had it here." Then she went back into her frantic search. We stood and waited. After a few more moments she looked up again and said, "I thought it would be safe in the box!" We had no idea what she was looking for.

Then Simone began to empty all the recipe boxes that Lucy had in the kitchen out onto the floor. We were amazed at how many index cards there were with hand written recipes on them. There was a collection spanning decades of cooking at Miss Lucy's restaurant. The expression on Samuel's face dramatically changed from concern to fright.

"Oh my, Lucy is gonna be mighty mad about this mess you are making. Oh my, how am I going to explain this to her when she gets back? Oh my, my."

Simone ignored him.

"There is only one last place to look," she said as she began to remove a floorboard just next to the stove. "There it is!" What she had discovered was Lucy's private collection of secret recipes in a tin box two times larger than all the others. "My sister guarded this box with her life. If it's anywhere it would be in here." We assumed she was referring to her own recipe box.

"She always said that this box would go to her grave with her." Simone stopped for a minute and for the first time looked at us directly and said, "No really, she wants to be buried with this box of recipes!"

When she opened the box and it was empty she started to laugh.

"Figures that my sister would think to take the contents of this box along with my Isabel off the island at the same time. Now I will never be able to claim what's mine. It is too late to turn back now. As my sister Lucy would say, let the devil be gone with his trouble. There is no time for that. No time at all!" Her laughter had suddenly changed to sobbing. She turned to us and said, "We need to go and Samuel you must promise to help me find that recipe box."

John and I knew she was serious. Before we left the restaurant, Simone spoke to Samuel.

"You must leave right now for St. Thomas and find that box. Once you find it, and I know you will, call Kiko and tell him you have what I needed. He'll know exactly what you are talking about. He will give you instructions as to what to do with it. Most importantly please make sure that Isabel and Lucy are safe and tell them both how much I love them."

We didn't ask Simone where we were going. She was in action mode and we knew her plan was now in high gear. Outside the restaurant and under the large table by the old sea grape tree we found three wet suits. We placed our valuables in an airtight bag, including the Vanity Fair magazine which was still in my hand. We walked quietly along the shoreline towards a rock where a small rubber dinghy was tied. Simone said, "You boys get in first and I'll push us off."

We didn't question her. "Okay," I whispered. Hope you know what you're doing." John then raised his index finger to his lips to instruct me to hush.

Simone smiled and said, "Let's hope I do."

We were out into deeper water when she gracefully pulled herself up with John's help. I held the dinghy steady with one of the oars. Once inside she started the motor and we headed towards Virgin Gorda. John and I were flanking her as we looked back in silence and saw Samuel's truck speeding away heading back towards town.

"Don't worry boys, I know where we're going and you're going to enjoy it as much as everything up until now." We then burst into laughter.

Simone had gotten us over to Virgin Gorda within twenty minutes. When we were far enough out into the darkness, we noticed some flashing lights at "Miss Lucy's". Figuring we had gone unnoticed and hoping the same for Samuel, we headed into the Baths, a collection of enormous boulders on the western tip of the island.

Simone led the way along the shoreline with the moon as our only source of light. Walking in close formation, with me in the middle, we saw the twinkle of tiny blue lights in the distance. John and I realized we were close to the small airstrip on the island. At about the time we reached the dirt tarmac, a baggage cart, aka golf cart, pulled up and the man driving it greeted Simone.

"Good evening Madame. Your jet is prepared and ready for takeoff." "Thank you," Simone said.

As we approached the jet we realized it was the very same one that had taken us back to New York from China. I knew that John was thinking the same thing I was. "Simone, is this yours?" She smiled, and suggested we take our wet suits off as soon as we boarded so as not to catch a chill.

"I have selected a few things that I think you both will like." Simone presented two cashmere robes. John turned to me as he received his. "You see I always told you that it is better to travel in style! Thank you, Simone." My jaw dropped.

"Aren't you going to say thank you", John said. I smiled and nodded a yes with my head.

After we changed we took our seats truly feeling like James Bond. As the jet was idling, an attendant, the same one from our return trip from China only days ago, offered us cocktails. Simone came out of the cabin suite after freshening up looking more beautiful than ever. As the three of us were settling in, John told us that he saw flashing red and blue lights in the distance. Simone looked out the window and instructed the pilot that it was time to leave.

The engines now in full firepower began moving the Gulfstream G550 over the short runway ahead. The jet had enough power to lift off under the circumstances, but the engines had to hit at least 15,000 RPM before the brakes were released providing enough thrust for lift given the short runway. As the engines revved up, police and lights were on the tarmac and heading toward us. Just as two of the vehicles came to a stop next to the jet, the pilot released the breaks. The thrust jolted our heads back pinning us to our seats. Thank goodness I had finished my drink. I looked outside and noticed more police cars were quickly approaching our jet when Simone looked over at us and casually said, “Good timing, oui?”

We were up some 25,000 feet in the air in no time at all. I asked Simone where we were going.

“Geneva,” Simone said. “We have business with some very influential people there. It will be very interesting, you’ll see.” John turned to me, “Like it hasn’t already been interesting.” Simone rang for more drinks.

Once we were all served, Simone raised her glass. "I'd like to say something." We raised our glasses.

"I am most thankful for you both. Without your companionship, I would never have been able to get this far. Everything was working out up until I couldn't find my old recipe box. John replied, "Maybe you won't need it." This time I raised my finger to politely suggest he hush.

Chapter Twenty-Three

"Family"

Samuel was instructed by Simone to go to St. Thomas and find the recipe box. When he did, and Simone was sure he would once he found Lucy, he was to call Kiko immediately. That's what he kept running through his mind as he drove over to Cruz Bay. He was hoping he'd find Jacko. He knew he could rely on Jacko's navigation skills to get him over to St. Thomas in record speed. He passed the local police as they headed down to "Miss Lucy's". He knew who they were looking for and hoped that he went unnoticed. Lucky for him Jacko was hanging out by the dock when he pulled into the parking lot.

"Jacko, just the man I was looking for."

"What brings you across the island now?"

"I need your help. I need to get to St. Thomas and find Lucy fast."

"No problem. Come aboard and let's go."

He started the twin engines and pulled out of the slip. Within minutes they were speeding ahead towards St. Thomas. Jacko was happy to help his friend without any questions. They arrived at Red Hook harbor within minutes.

"Do you want me to wait for you?"

"No. I should be fine."

"No problem, but I'll be hanging here all night just in case."

"Thanks, Jacko."

Samuel made his way to the house where Lucy and Isabel were staying. From the bottom of the road he saw the porch lights on and was confident that they were at home. As he stepped onto the old rickety porch the creaking sounds from the floorboards alerted those inside that someone was outside. The second Samuel reached the screen door he was met by Lucy with arms folded across her breasts.

"What in the Lord's name are you doing here?"

"Aren't you going to let me in?"

"Not until you tell me what business brings you here."

"I came to talk to you."

"About what?"

"Our sister Simone."

Lucy at that point told Isabel who was seated in an old wicker chair inside to go into the kitchen to help her cousin wash the supper dishes.

"Happy to see you and Isabel are doing fine here with cousin."

"Stop the chit chat. Now what do you want?"

"I told you. It's about Simone."

"Be gone with that devil talk."

"Now are you going to let me in to talk civil or do I need to tear down this door and make you?"

Samuel was losing his patience and for the first time he raised his voice. Lucy knew that for him to get to this point it must be important.

"I'll come out and join you on the porch. You wait while I check on things in the kitchen."

"Thank you."

"Fine. I'm only doing this to save me from having to replace a screen door."

Lucy turned away and walked towards the kitchen while Samuel settled into one of the two rocking chairs on the porch and looked out to the water. While he waited, he thought about how he should approach the topic of the recipe box. He already felt a sense of accomplishment having gotten this far with Lucy, but he knew time wasn't on his side and needed to get her to come around quickly.

"Now what's this all about? Showing up here unannounced and this late to boot. You already know how I feel about that sister of ours, never did nothing for anyone but herself. All those years I looked after her and what did I get, nothing but trouble. The best thing that came from that girl is Isabel. That's right. That child was a gift from above and she need not know anything about her past. Do you hear me?'

Samuel suddenly stood up and faced Lucy.

"Enough of that talk. I have listened to you, taken orders from you, tried to please you for longer that I can even remember. And what thanks did I ever get from you?

Tell me sister, what thanks? Now I am going to do some talking and you are going to sit there and do some listening. Do you hear me?"

Lucy, rather stunned, looked up at her brother and smiled.

"Well, well, look who is now finally wearing the pants in the family. Maybe there is still hope for you after all."

"Don't you get all smart on me Lucy. I need to talk to you and you need to try and understand what I'm telling you."

"Go ahead little brother I'm listening."

Samuel sat on the edge of the porch with his back resting on the post as he faced Lucy.

"I don't know all the answers or even the reason why things between us ended up this way. You tried your best to manage a situation that was beyond our control. I am so grateful that you were strong enough, smart enough and caring enough to keep the three of us together after Mama's passing. I know it wasn't easy growing up so fast and being burdened at such a young age."

Lucy suddenly lowered her arms and folded her hands on her lap.

"You know we love you for that and even if you never heard it from us, and I speak for Simone too, I mean it."

The hard expression on her face softened.

"I know that we should have said this to you a long time ago, but life sometimes doesn't reveal things in a timely way. Thing is, me and Simone, well mostly Simone can really use your help. You see, she is trying to do good. She knows that her past has caused you pain, but it caused her a lot more pain than you know. The thing is she don't want her past to mess up her future with Isabel. I know that for a fact because not only have I talked to her but I've seen her just today."

Lucy's expression changed again in reaction to the mention of Simone's name. It wasn't a pleasant one.

"Now, can you please just put aside your bad feelings about her for a minute and try to understand what is going on here?"

"I'm not sure I want to." Lucy looked away from him.

"You know just as well as I do that the time would come that Isabel would need to find out about who her real mama is. I know you don't want to hear that, but down deep you know that it is true. We lost our Mama too early. Let's not do the work of God and take Isabel's mother away from her."

She looked back at him and he saw in her eyes that he had gotten through to her.

"What do you want me to do?"

"Lucy, why did you take Simone's recipe box? You don't even know why she wants it, neither do I but she does. Where is it? Whatever it is I trust that Simone is trying to make things right and you and me, we need to help her. We are family, the only family I have, we have."

Taken back by what Samuel had just said, Lucy stood up and joined him on the edge of the porch facing him.

"Why Lucy, is that a tear I see running down your cheek?"

"You know it is. So, don't be asking me a foolish question. Do you hear me boy!"

They sat outside for some time. Lucy listened as Samuel explained that Simone had gone to the restaurant only a couple of hours ago, avoiding of course telling her what a mess she made of the place.

"Whatever it is, I know she needs that box."

Lucy said she had it and called out to Isabel to bring it to her outside.   Samuel went inside and called Kiko.

"Child, we need to do something.

"Yes, ma'am."

"That's a good girl. Auntie Lucy has a lot to share with you, some good, some not, but in the end, you need to know about things from the past that will help you understand the things that are happening now. Now go inside and wash up."

Chapter Twenty-Four

"Freefall"

We rested for a few hours but were interrupted by a message from our pilot that we were being followed by the United States Air Force.

"Are you sure?"

"Yes Madame. They have been trailing us ever since we flew over Greenland."

"Do you think they know our destination?"

"It's most likely, Madame. We needed to file our flight plan in Virgin Gorda prior to take off."

"Do you think we can lose them?"

"Not likely, Madame. Their jets are designed for this kind of thing."

"I see. Do you think we could divert and land in Milan?"

"I can check with air traffic at Malpensa. Please give me a moment, Madame."

"Yes, thank you."

Simone was now sure the US Air Force knew our destination and decided it was time for drastic measures (as if this unexpected flight wasn't enough, I thought). She explained that we would enter Geneva by way of a train from Milan if we got clearance to land there. After conferring with the pilot the plan was aborted. It seemed that the airport control would not permit the private jet to land on such short notice since it was not deemed an emergency. Simone began to think about an alternate plan.

"We need to create some type of diversion to confuse them."

"While we are in mid-air?"

"Oui! I have it."

Simone smiled and then got up from her seat to speak to the captain.

When Simone suggested an airdrop I almost fainted. The thought of jumping from a moving jet was more than I could imagine doing for anything or anyone. Jumping from this altitude was beyond my capacity. I mean, I am afraid to climb up a ladder unless John is standing on the ground holding it. John, however, was all for it. He turned to me and told me not to worry and that he would help me.

"You'll be fine. Just keep your eyes on me and wait until I pull my cord then you do the same."

"Are you out of your mind?" I finished the rest of my drink in one gulp.

"It's easy", he said and then started to laugh.

That's when Simone took my hand and said, "No, no. Not us. I was thinking of the crew aboard who are skilled in this type of thing. They are former members of the security forces, Cloud View, and are highly trained for nighttime sky diving." Simone then laughed.

"I only have these shoes with me, my Jimmy's! Not the right shoe for sky diving!"

There were six of us on board the Gulfstream, the three of us and the three crew members. To create a distraction, we needed two of the crew to jump. The captain agreed with Simone's theory that if the jet trailing us saw three people jump, hopefully they would think it was us and head over to the private airstrip near Lake Como to wait for instructions to apprehend us. I thought it made sense since it was us that they were after but with only two sky diving they might think that the one person they were after, which was Simone, might still be onboard our jet.

The captain asked Simone, “What about a third person to provide the impression that it is you three jumping? Simone said, “We won’t need a third.”

John and I were confused along with the captain. While the jet rushed toward the lake Simone explained what she was thinking.

“They will see three leap from the jet but only two of the parachutes will open. We need to assume that they will think the third has malfunctioned and became an unfortunate victim of the fall. Prepare a flight suit with the necessary gear attached. We will insert the remaining bottles of Cristal champagne to weigh it so that it falls in the right direction with a great deal of style.”

I almost complained about how it was going to be a waste of good champagne but under the circumstances I thought better of it.

As we approached Lake Como our jet began to descend with the goal to level off at 10,000 feet. Simone, in the meantime, called her friend George who had a villa on the lake to inform him of unexpected guests. She asked if he would stand ready with his boat out on the lake and look for the drop off. He assured Simone that for her he would do anything. "I'll take very good care of your friends tonight. Don't you worry."

AT 10,000 feet, "Cristal" was suited up and ready for her jump. Simone turned to the captain and navigator who were escorting the champagne dummy to thank them.

"I will remember this forever."

Without missing a beat, the navigator replied, "Remember this as well, a good martini is the one that is always there when you need it!" I thought to myself how right you are.

The pilot slowed the jet down, causing the US Air Force jet to do the same. We anxiously hoped that at this point they would take the bait.

"Good luck and we will see you in Geneva." The navigators' voice echoed in free fall. We watched the three holding hands as they headed down to the lake below. The dramatic feat was buffered with a laugh about the prospect of Cristal heading right into the arms of George waiting below.

Chapter Twenty-Five

"Final Descent"

The decoy over Lake Cuomo worked. We had managed to throw off the Air Force jet trailing us. We watched it change course on the radar screen. It was heading for the private airstrip within miles of the lake. We hoped the crew, including Cristal, landed safely with George nearby to pick them up. We would only know that once we were in Geneva.

Our new pilot kept a close eye on the radar to ensure that we were in the clear. With the potential interception gone our anxiety shifted as we came closer and closer to our destination. Eventually Simone told us to prepare for arrival. She also suggested that we have one last cocktail before landing.

"We will need a drink to provide us company as we dress, something I had learned while reading about Vreeland and her husband Reed. It was a ritual of theirs."

"Of course, Robert and I always referred to their expression of having a 'dressing cocktail'.

"Yes, exactly right. I asked the navigator to shake a few before he jumped and viola, here that are," Simone said as she carried the tray of drinks from the galley and told us that in the forward cabin were two garment bags for us.

"Please help yourself to the martinis and nibbles and then we should go ahead and get ready. I will dress here. Please join me when you are ready."

John excused us and we went to the cabin to change. After a few sips I turned to John and asked, "What did we do throughout all of this to help Simone? I mean, we only have been here without really doing much to aid her".

Turning to me he said, "Not sure, but perhaps being here was all she needed".

Then John handed me one of the two garment bags and said we should hurry and change and get back to the salon to join Simone.

Opening the garment bag with my name on it I discovered a very fine suit. Inside the jacket's breast pocket was a monogram in silk, my first name. It was a handmade suit from the House of Tom Ford. We both found a note inside the breast pocket of the jacket.

A suit is made from cloth, the design is from inspiration, and its style comes from the man who wears it. Enjoy, Tom.

"Who doesn't she know?" John smiled and told me to hurry up.

Dressed in our new suits, we entered the cabin to find Simone dressed in a blue grey silk Chanel dress. Her hair was now pulled back as sleek and elegant as she. On her neck was the only sign of jewelry, a platinum chain with a single charm. It was a crystal vile, something that we hadn't noticed her wearing earlier.

Simone asked us to sit beside her. "I want to tell you something that is very important." She began to talk as the captain informed us we now had ten minutes before our descent into the Geneva International Airport.

"My dear friends," Simone began to say, "You see, it is because of you, that I now understand the meaning of this charm resting on my neck." She held it up to us then gently wrapped her hand around it. Without moving her hand, she told us that it was from the Doctor. He had given it to her in Paris the day before they were to return to St. John for the birth of Isabel.

"He told me to always keep it close, to protect it for it held the future promise for our child and for all children. At the time, I had no idea what he was talking about, but I have never taken it off since that night."

Simone then removed her hand from the crystal and put her hands in ours, "Today is the first time that I understand its value. It is Laramar." She paused and wiped a tear from her eye.

"It is a blue stone found in the Caribbean that captures the color of the sea and sky. A stone used for healing. The powerful energy it contains summons all that is positive in nature. It has an ability to connect the emotional with the physical when it is used by stimulating the heart and providing internal wisdom. Laramar is a spiritual catalyst and with all the changes happening around us, it's importance is greater now more than ever."

John and I were mesmerized by Simone's explanation of what was inside the crystal vial hanging from her neck. It was beautiful and if you looked at it closely you could indeed see the colors of the sea and sky.

"You may be wondering why it is only now that I understand this. It's simple. It is because of you two. You entered my life, a world that you knew little about, but your courage and compassion for goodness reawakened something in me." Simone paused and John handed her a handkerchief to wipe the tears from her cheek.

"After our first meeting, I sensed that the Doctor sent you to me. Your conversations with Samuel confirmed that. Samuel, my dear trusting brother, who witnessed a love become something that I was forced to hide. I vowed to my husband over his breathless body on that night, the night that our child was taken by my sister Lucy, that I would make things right. I have not been responsible in living up to that promise." She paused for a moment and looked out the window. In the distance were the lights of the city. John leaned forward and held her hand.

"It was your compassion, and my brother's love, that has awakened my sense of duty to fulfill that promise. I saw in your eyes on our first night in Paris kindness. I am grateful that you reached out, giving me strength. It was because of you that I called Samuel to talk. And it is because of that call we are here to do what needs to be done. It is what the Doctor always wanted, to make a better life for all and for he to be understood." Tears began to roll down her face.

"I cannot thank you more for your trust. What is about to take place will change us, and it is you that I thank for that. When we arrive in Geneva, we must stay close. Kiko already told me that there will be quite a bit of excitement and I can think of no one who I would rather be with for this adventure than you two."

I got the answer to my question of why us. This was an unexpected adventure but one that I knew I would treasure for the rest of my life.

"Madame Oppenheimer we are cleared for descent," said the captain. "Please secure your positions for landing."

Twenty-Six

"Safe Landing"

Flashing lights greeted our arrival into the Geneva International Airport. The demonstrations now amounting to over 600,000 marchers spread through the city. The protestors were there to demand action from the leaders of the nations around the world who had gathered in Geneva for this meeting. Members of the international press were standing by at the airport reporting on who next would be arriving from the list of luminaires they had obtained. The arrival of Dr. J Robert Oppenheimer's widow was the one that seemed to interest them the most.

The jet came to a stop and security vehicles ambushed us within seconds. We sat on the runway for what seemed like an eternity until the captain entered the cabin and said we had approval to disembark. Simone stood, checked her hair then turned to us and said, "It's time."

As we walked down the staircase attached to the jet, we were overwhelmed with the number of press and security personnel waiting below.

Simone turned back to us and said, "Remember, keep calm and stick close together".

We followed the assigned guard one by one on a narrow path flanked by security. Kiko was standing by the car waiting for us. Pandemonium ensued around us. John assumed that security clearance had been pre-arranged, as we were never asked to provide our passports which helped make for a swift exit from the airport.

"This way, Simone. The Council is just about to begin." Kiko said.

Once inside the car he looked back at us, winked and said, "You are safe, and by the way, welcome to Geneva gentlemen, it is nice to see you again."

"Kiko, did my brother speak to you?" Simone asked. He turned around and told her that yes, they spoke and not to worry, everything is going to work out just fine.

"No not just fine, better than that. Everything is going to be brilliant, you'll see." He then turned around and gave the driver instructions to get us to the Council compound quickly.

"When you arrive at the destination make sure you keep close together. Do not look to your left or right, only ahead and do not allow anyone to stop you and try to talk about your business here." Kiko then exited the car and was escorted to a waiting limo that would take him to the Council ahead of us.

We drove through the hordes of cameras and TV crew vehicles and onto a road that was lined with security forces as far as the eye could see. Simone looked over toward us and said, "Our arrival seems to be a big deal".

The driver explained to us that we would be entering the World Council of Nations compound by way of a security driveway not accessible to the press. As we got closer to the compound he called security and was told they were not allowing anyone entry using the security driveway given the unexpected activity outside the Council grounds.

"Are you kidding? The road leading to the front entrance is a mad house. Are you sure we don't have clearance to enter the compound from the alternate entrance as we were told?"

"Sorry, mate. We need to close the alt entrance down given the chaos on the side street and fear that the entire compound would potentially have a security breach."

"Will there be back up for us at the main entrance? We are almost at the first check point for the drop."

"Yes, mate. Don't worry. We have security at the main gate. You should not have a problem. Over and out."

We would need to enter the compound through the main gate. When we reached that side of the compound there was mayhem. There were no security forces in sight.

"This is about as far as I can get. The protestors are blocking the road and I am concerned that if I agitate the crowd things will get out of control.

"How far are we from the main gate?" Simone asked.

"We are only about 10 feet from the gate. If you look up you can see the flag at the top of the gate post. I am sure the security force will be standing by to get you in quickly and without incident."

“Okay. We will get out here and keep our eye on the flag.”

“Yes, Madame and by the way may I say it was my pleasure and honor to have escorted you this far.”

“You are very kind. If you can stand by in case we have an issue...”

“That was always my intention Madame. I am certain everything will be just fine.”

We waited until our driver got word that the security detail at the main gate was ready for us. The mob scene outside reminded me of the movie ‘Day of the Locust’. I kept thinking what’s going to happen when the driver opens the door?

Quickly the door opened, and the driver helped Simone out of the car. The driver stood in front of Simone as John and I slid across the seat and out onto the pavement. Suddenly the crowd of press realized it was the widow of the famous Dr. Oppenheimer. The security forces were being challenged to hold the path open as the crowd began to swell behind them.

John insisted that he go first, reminding us not to look anywhere but forward, and under no circumstance were we to stop. “Look up at the flag, that’s the direction we need to head in.”

The flashes from the cameras that surrounded us were going off like fireworks on the 4th of July. John shouted, “hold tight and heads up”. Within seconds, we were being wedged between the people on both sides of the pathway. Looking ahead the lights of the compound became dim as we were crushed by the masses around us.

“Keep walking! Keep walking! Keep your eyes on the flag!”, John kept repeating to us.

To my horror, I felt Simone’s hand begin to slip from my grasp. Holding tightly to her fingertips it was a struggle as she began to be swallowed by the hordes of people. I tried to keep a hand on hers but it was snapped away. John had reached the gate holding my hand, pulling forward as the gate opened only inches to let us in. I turned to see if she was behind us.

“Simone! Simone!”, I shouted.

Then I let go of John's hand to find Simone. She emerged with the help of the security guards and was reaching for my hand.

"Simone here! Simone, grab my hand!", I yelled through the crowd.

The unruly crowd began to separate us again, but I never stopped looking at Simone. I began swinging my arms as if I were shooing flies and shouted, "No! Leave her alone!"

I pushed everybody out of my way to reach her. John held the gate open with one hand and reached out for mine with his other. I found Simone and grabbed her waist. Holding her close I said, "This way Madame O."

Chapter Twenty-Seven

"Circle of Nations"

We managed to pass through the gates leading to the entrance of the headquarters of the World Council of Nations with the help of the security force. The assistant to the Minister of Human Compassion was now at the front steps waiting to escort us into the hall. In contrast to what was going on outside, the interior of the building was in perfect order.

"Welcome to the WCN, Madame Oppenheimer and colleagues," said the assistant to the Minister. "We are most honored and grateful that you are here. Please follow me to the antechamber of the Circle of Nations."

"Of course. But first I must make a phone call."

"That's fine, there's time before the Council is ready to see you." We waited with the assistant until Simone returned from making her call.

Simone returned within a few minutes.

"I called George to find out if Cristal made it to the boat."

We smiled and asked what he said.

"George said that Cristal and he got well acquainted last night. Shall we go?"

We waited in the antechamber to the Circle of Nations during which time we observed in silence the activity going on. The one-way mirror allowed us to see into the circular room. The walls were at least forty feet tall and at the ceiling was a circular ring of lights. In the center of the room was a round steel table where the various representatives of the World Council of Nations had seats. There were over 200 people around the diameter of the table, representing every nation on the planet. Behind the round table were rows of chairs where members of the WCN would observe only. Only those seated around the table were permitted to speak. A singular voice from each country. Along the walls were projected visuals of the catastrophic activities occurring around the globe. Droughts in Africa, revolution in Egypt, all interspersed with images of famine and plague in a variety of countries.

I stood between John and Simone watching the visuals of the devastation occurring around our planet, including the disorder going on outside the WCN in Geneva.

The assistant told us that the purpose of this display was to make members of the WCN aware of world issues. Those seated at the table had taken a vow on behalf of their nation to bring all human suffering to an end. I was shocked to learn that the images were a live feed from the various locations. As the lights in the room dimmed, the disturbing visuals morphed into a spectacular panoramic visual of blue water. Silence enveloped the room. The swirling blue waves dissolved and were replaced by words in every language representing the members of the Council. From a podium in the center of the room the WCN Speaker called for attention.

"Members of the WCN, welcome to the forum on the most recent crisis to be addressed this evening. Remember all gathered that our mission is to end human suffering. The need for clean water is at crisis levels across the globe. We will discuss this and we will decide the proper course of action. It is our duty as nations of the world to vote on a solution and end this epidemic now."

The room remained silent and the blue waves reappeared dissolving into images of the drought and pollution making the access to fresh water impossible in areas on our planet. The images evaporated once again into a globe indicating where the need for clean water was at peak levels: Nicaragua, Bolivia, Sierra Leone, Kenya, India, Egypt, and even parts of the United States, Russia and China. Facts of the impact of the crisis appeared on the chamber wall:

- 6,000 children under the age of five die daily due to contaminated water.
- 1.1 billion people have inadequate access to safe drinking water.
- Water-related diseases are the single largest cause of human sickness.
- Women and children spend up to six hours a day collecting water.
- Climate changes are affecting weather patterns causing excessive draughts in some countries and flooding in others.

The information and images continued to rotate around the chamber in a multitude of languages for all to read and understand. The facts could not be ignored by anyone seated in the room. The purpose, the assistant told us, was to engage every country present. They had the power to decide the outcome of the discussion and the fate of those in dire need of water to survive.

John turned to me and asked if I noticed that the pitchers of water on the round table, once holding crystal clear water were now dark after council aides injected pollutants into them with plastic syringes. It was a demonstration of what a large part of the world's population was dealing with. No one seated would even consider drinking from the pitchers now in front of them.

The images stopped and the Speaker of the Chamber introduced the countries that were now involved in providing a solution to the horrific epidemic. The Speaker then requested the following countries enter the center of the chamber.

"The Republic of China, The Republic of France, The United States of America, if you please. It is time for the council to consider your solutions for this situation. Please present your solution."

The lighting in the chamber dimmed, except for the ring of lights directly over the steel round table. The room was silent as representatives from the nations called stepped into the circle. The representative from France did not step forward.

"Is the representative of the Republic of France present? The council is requesting the representatives of France to come to the inner circle."

There was silence in the Chamber.

The Speaker repeated the message a second time. The French representative of the WCN seated leaned into the microphone in front of him.

"Pardon moi, Madames and Messieurs. France is unable to participate in this evening's discussion. We regret to inform the members of the WCN that we do not have the required data to participate. Our data source, Blue Water International, has refused to cooperate." The U.S representative then spoke.

"This is most unfortunate in light of the recent indictment alleging Blue Water and their poor filtration standards. We are not surprised by your decision to withdraw and feel that as a result you should forfeit your vote this evening."

The Speaker interrupted the representative from the U.S., requesting that he refrain from any further comments. He then addressed the French representative.

"Why is the WCN being informed about this now?"

The representative from France stood and confirmed what the U.S representative had just said was true.

"We are most sorry for this rather unfortunate situation. We realized 24 hours ago that our process for the conversion of polluted water into fresh water, conducted by Blue Water International, only provides sixty percent filtration. Thus, allowing forty percent of the contaminates to remain in the newly filtered water. The filtrated water, we fear, remains potentially deadly."

The expression on the face of the representative from China seated at the table was one of complete shock.

A growing rumble in the room began in reaction to the information provided by the French.

The Speaker attempted to bring order to the Chamber.

"I call this meeting to order! Ladies and Gentlemen of the Council! France has withdrawn its participation in the discussion this evening due to unfortunate circumstances."

When calm in the Chamber was restored the Speaker introduced the two remaining participating nations.

"We call our attention to the members of China, and the United States, who have been patiently waiting while France provided us with their explanation. Will the scientist representing both please begin the discussion?"

Both scientist stepped forward and the circular flooring below them ascended 5 feet in the air to provide a clear view to the entire chamber gathered. The cylinder platform was now illuminated by spotlights above. Rising from within the platform were three laboratory stations. Two were manned by the two countries present and one was left vacant. The Speaker took his place and introduced the participants.

"Members of the World Council of Nations may I present to you the lead scientist from China, Dr. Wu, and from the United States, Dr. Williams."

John and I looked at each other while Simone focused on Dr. Wu.

"Gentlemen the forum is now yours. Have you decided which of the two nations will begin this evening's discussion?" Dr. Williams volunteered to go first. He stepped into the center of the platform.

With all eyes on him he began to address the Chamber.

"It is with a great responsibility that we, The United States of America, have come before you with our thoughts for restoring a fundamental need of all, access to clean and safe water. It is no surprise to many of you that we consider our nation as the guardian of lesser countries on this planet. We were the first to land a man on the moon some 50 years ago. We were the first to encourage a nuclear nonproliferation treaty with Russia during the Cold

War. Even today, we continue to lead the way in advancing peace efforts in the Middle East."

The doctor took a step forward appearing unnerved by the focus on him. I was in awe that this was the same man who visited us not too long ago. His demeanor then was suspicious, here in Geneva he appeared to be dangerous.

"We realize that war has and always will stem from the need to secure basic human needs. Nations still fight over land and invade borders to dominate resources. The architects of war know no wrong, they only know gain."

There was a sense of anxiety filtering into the Chamber as Dr. William continued.

"Today our aging planet is providing less and less for us to conquer. We have managed to deplete our planet of most of its natural resources. The World Council of Nations is aware of our planet's current crises. I will present a plan that will provide a solution to our water resource issue. This plan will allow access to those who choose clean water."

The Speaker interrupted Dr. Williams.

"If you please, Dr. Williams. I believe we are gathered here today to understand your nations proposal. I think we can all agree that we are indebted to the United States for its continuous care and guidance, however, the agenda today is less about expressing our collective gratitude and more about a plan to address the world issue on today's agenda."

Dr. Williams smiled.

"We are close to the solution, as we have spent years applying research from Dr. Oppenheimer's notes and his earlier studies on the issue. We have reached the final stages in our experimentation and believe we are within weeks of having the solution."

Dr. Williams was interrupted again by the Speaker.

"Dr. Williams, can you clarify what you mean by allow access to those who *choose* clean water? I hope this isn't an attempt to discriminate between those who are allowed access from those who are not. I apologize in advance if I have misunderstood."

Dr. Williams looking directly at the Speaker responded.

"Sir, no need to apologize. You have completely captured the exactness of my words. I have been instructed by the U.S. government to be very clear on this point."

The remark created a roar in the Circle of Nations Chamber. The entire room was now in total chaos. Dr. Williams who seemed unfazed by the reaction returned to the lab station. The Speaker tried to maintain decorum. We now knew why Dr. Williams made his visit and was so intent on getting whatever information he could out of us. His transparency on stage underscored our mistrust from the moment he left our apartment that night.

"Order in the chamber! Order I say! Will all the members of the council please settle down immediately! We must have order in the chamber! Will you please be seated. Order I say!"

It took nearly 10 minutes to bring the Chamber to order before the Speaker spoke.

"Dr. Williams, on behalf of the World Council of Nations, we thank you for being so very honest with your current administration's agenda. However, we as a collective of concerned nations are not gathered here to profit from this epidemic. We as a Council are here for a humanitarian purpose, to find a universal solution and make it available to all."

The Speaker entered the center of the circle and spoke directly to Dr. Williams.

"Dr. Williams, I am certain you will not find any support for your plan here in Geneva. Kindly take your seat."

Chapter Twenty-Eight

"H2O"

After a standing ovation by the entire audience in the room, for the dismissal of Dr. Williams, the Speaker called the Chamber back to order.

"Order in the chamber! Order in the chamber! We will now proceed with the discussion led by China. Dr. Wu, are you prepared for the discussion and demonstration?"

Doctor Wu smiled and nodded. The chamber, now completely silent, waited for him to speak. He adjusted the microphone and began.

"Members of the WCN, we in China are aware of this crisis as it is now at epidemic proportions in our nation. We are shocked and greatly concerned by the recent news regarding the inadequacies of Blue Water International."

His voice lowered.

"They have been a major supplier of water within many parts of our nation for some time now. With the exposure of their duplicity we, all of us, must be even more committed to now finding a solution."

Dr. Wu became silent, cupped his hands in front of him and looked down for a moment as if he was praying. Looking up he searched for Dr. Williams and spoke directly to him seated with the others in the Chamber.

"Many years ago, I had the pleasure of working at Columbia University with Dr. Oppenheimer. Our purpose was to find a way to transform sea water into a source of drinking water. The process of desalination, if you will, makes that which could not be consumed palatable."

Simone smiled knowing that Dr. Wu was about to reveal what she knew would be the beginning of the needed solution that her husband and he worked so hard to discover.

"This experimentation was more complex than we first thought. We, Dr. Oppenheimer and myself, needed to explore precise measurements that provided the transformation."

I looked up and realized that Simone knew exactly where Dr. Wu was going with his presentation.

"Our studies ended abruptly when I was, to put it politely, encouraged to return to China to continue on my own with the experimentation. This unforeseen situation ended all contact with my colleagues at Columbia, especially with the late Dr. Oppenheimer."

The Chamber responded with nods and light applause.

"I have had many years to consider the damages to those in dire need that this action by my own government caused. However, I would like to believe, even today as I stand before you, that our country has learned from our past mistakes and is now committed no matter what, to finding a solution."

The tone of Dr. Wu's voice now indicated that his emotions were beginning to surface. Dr. Wu looked over at the representative from China seated at the table when the Speaker spoke.

"Dr. Wu, do you have a solution?"

Then came the response from Dr. Wu.

"Members of the Council, China has the basic formula for the solution to end the global shortage of potable water. May I attempt our demonstration before the audience present here at the Chamber of Nations?"

Doctor Wu stood at the laboratory station in the inner circle. The two vacant stations designated for France and the United States were a reminder that neither country had anything to offer as a solution to this global epidemic.

John asked Simone if the laboratory set up in front of Dr. Wu was like the one she saw in Shanghai?

"Yes, exactly."

I then asked if she thought it would work.

"Let's hope so," Simone said and took a step closer to the glass partition that separated us from those present in the Chamber.

Dr. Wu ignited the burner placed on the laboratory table. At the station was a larger beaker, which the doctor explained was filled with salt water. The contents were confirmed by an agent of the Council. Dr. Wu placed the beaker on the flame and we watched the liquid inside begin to bubble. The liquid inside the beaker was at a full boil when the doctor placed a thermometer inside to check the temperature. The thermometer read four hundred degrees Fahrenheit. It was then that Simone turned to us.

"No. It will not work. He does not remember what the final ingredient is as the catalyst."

The doctor checked the temperature again as it had reached five hundred degrees. Simone pulled her cell phone from her Kelly bag and phoned Kiko.

"Kiko, he needs my help. I have the answer that the World Council of Nations is searching for. May I please be escorted into the chamber?"

Dr. Wu was now tapping the beaker with the hopes that the solvent inside would transform into the required solution needed.

"Of course. This is the moment that we have waited for. I will send for you at once."

After minutes watching the bubbling contents in the beaker, Dr. Wu lowered his head and requested permission to leave the inner circle.

The Speaker then responded.

"Dr. Wu, you have proven to us that your intentions are honorable. We at the World Council appreciate your effort here tonight. Are you sure you wouldn't like to try onc more time?"

Dr. Wu looked up and said.

"Unfortunately, no."

The room remained silent. The Speaker was just about to suggest a 15-minute recess when he was interrupted by the assistant to the Minister of Human Compassion.

"Members of the Council, Madame Oppenheimer, who as most of you know is here with us has volunteered to assist Dr. Wu. With the permission of the Speaker, may we request she enter the center platform and assist?"

A rumble of excited voices echoed around the circular room. Only a handful of the people in the room had met her, but they all knew that she was not only a luminary, but luminous as she entered the chamber. I looked over to where Dr. Williams was seated and from the expression on his face I could surmise he was not pleased that this was happening.

"If the members of the Council would be kind enough to allow Madame Oppenheimer to enter the Circle of Nations."

We wished her luck and then were lead from the antechamber into the Chamber by security guards to chairs behind the circular table reserved for visiting VIP's. Inside the scale of the room seemed even larger than I expected. Simone stepped into the center of the Circle of Nations and ascended onto the platform by the staircase provided. The Speaker officially acknowledged her presence and introduced her to those present.

"Welcome Madame Oppenheimer to the World Council of Nations. We are honored to have you join us. As is protocol for the Circle of Nations, please state your full name and inform us as to which country you represent."

The question asked was translated into multiple languages for the members of the Council.

"My name is Simone Oppenheimer."

"Which country do you represent, if you please?"

"For the purposes of today, I do not represent any country."

A hum of voices now filtered around the room.

"Madame Oppenheimer, can you please explain what you mean? It is protocol that guests of the Council identify which country they represent for proceedings such as this."

Simone then stepped forward to address the Council with an air of unwavering confidence.

"If the Council pleases I will explain."

The room was silent.

"I represent a man who felt he was forsaken by his country. A man shamed and retreated into self-exile when I met him. My love for him did not understand this abandonment by his country. My love believed in his goodness." Simone paused for a moment then looked directly at the U.S. representative seated at the table of the Circle of Nations.

"I represent Dr. Julius Robert Oppenheimer. A man abandoned after having given so much to the world. I am here to restore his name and the future of our child and the children of this planet who need his gift now more than ever before. My name is Madame Oppenheimer."

From above the chamber the Minister of Human Compassion spoke.

"Will the Chamber please accept from this woman a final demonstration and consider the potential solution?"

The entire Chamber began to applaud and began shouting, "Madame Oppenheimer, Madame Oppenheimer…."

Simone then addressed the Chamber.

"I have come to better understand the loneliness of the scientist and the artist as both live in a compartmentalized world. Discoveries are sometimes not for the good or benefit of all."

The Chamber was in complete awe of her at this point.

"Does the inventor know that his invention may not benefit the masses when he begins his creative voyage?"

The chorus of voices expressed a unified understanding of her words.

"Is the scientist devastated by the negative impact of his passion when he learns that his creativity did not serve in a good way?"

There were sounds of support raising from those present.

"He devoted his life to those things that would benefit all."

The members of the Council applauded and as it echoed throughout the chamber Simone graciously asked for them to stop.

"May I introduce, again, Dr. Wu?" The doctor now stood behind the laboratory table for the second time. "He has waited a very long time for this moment." Simone whispered into his ear.

Dr. Wu ignited the beaker for a second time. When the water in the beaker reached the required temperature of five hundred degrees Fahrenheit, Dr. Wu turned to Simone and requested her help. Simone stood over the beaker and took from her neck the crystal vial. She unscrewed the top of the vial and poured the essential catalyst, a pinch of Laramar, into the boiling salt water. Within moments the beaker began to foam and bubble over. What remained in the beaker was pure water. It was done. The chamber exploded in cheers.

The Minister of Human Compassion, Kiko Foo now spoke.

"Please! Order in the chamber! Please let us have order in the chamber. Please, can we have order!"

Simone looked out at us standing in the room.

"Thank you, Madame Oppenheimer and Dr. Wu for your successful demonstration."

Dr. Wu and Simone were now in the center of the inner circle. They embraced and the Council members in the chamber continued to cheer, ignoring the request from the Minister for order. Simone then reached out both hands to us in gratitude for us being there. After order was restored in the chamber Kiko asked if there were any questions from those in the Circle of Nations. The chamber went silent.

"Are there any questions for Dr. Wu or Madame Oppenheimer?" Kiko repeated, "Questions?"

Dr. Williams, seated at the Circle of Nations, spoke.

"Madame Oppenheimer, may I ask where you were born?"

Simone answered St. John Virgin Island.

"Madame, isn't that a territory of the United States?"

"Yes, it is."

"Yes, it is, Madame Oppenheimer. As such, doesn't that make you an official citizen of the United States of America?"

The room was aware of where this questioning was going.

"Yes sir, as you have indicated that makes me officially a citizen of the United States of America."

"Very good." Dr. Williams responded in a snarky tone.

"Do you have proof, perhaps a patent, that indicates ownership of this formula?"

"Sir, I do have a document from my late husband."

"Wonderful. Can you please provide us with it now?"

"I do not have it with me, but it does exist."

Dr. Williams stood up and turned to the members of the Council and said,

"Without the documented proof of individual ownership, the United States of America stakes claim to the formula as demonstrated here this evening."

The Chamber burst into loud objection to what Dr. Williams had said. He continued above the noise.

"Under the charter of the WCN and I quote, 'The participation by any individual within the Council is recognized only by country and not by the individual status', end of quote. Furthermore, it is stated that any speaker, and in this case, I cite one Madame Oppenheimer, invited into the Circle of Nations is considered a representative of the country where they are a citizen. What this means Madame is that without proof of individual ownership, the patent for this formula is the property of the United States."

Simone looked over at the two of us horrified at what she was hearing.

Dr. Williams turned to address the Speaker of the Chamber.

"The United States of America claims ownership to this formula given the fact that Madame Oppenheimer has not provided proof of individual ownership and is by birth a citizen of our country."

Outrage resounded within the circular wall. The Speaker then asked,

"Madame Oppenheimer, if you please, what is your country of residence?"

"I am a citizen of the United States of America."

"Do you realize that as a resident of the United States of America, and in accordance with the WCN guidelines your efforts and this formula are under the jurisdiction of your government?"

The Chamber sat in anticipated silence waiting for her response.

"I understand that, Your Honor."

"This of course is part of the WCN guidelines. If you can produce any support of your claim we will be able to accept it; however, without it we must follow the rules of the WCN."

Simone became anxious and took a moment to collect her thoughts.

"Documented proof does exist but I was unable to find it before my trip here to Geneva. I hope that the Circle of Nations will grant me a short period of time to locate it."

Looking down at Dr. Williams now seated at the table Simone spoke directly to him.

"I stand before you not as a citizen of the United States, but as an individual representing a man who believed that like oxygen, ideas are free."

Her statement created an uproar in the Chamber of Nations.

Dr. Williams stood and spoke directly to Simone.

"Madame Oppenheimer, do you think that we will allow our work at Columbia University for the past 25 years to end here with your Save the Children rhetoric?"

There were strong negative reactions by all present to his remark but he continued in even a louder manner.

"We will ask you one last time before the Circle of Nations and under the bylaws of this organization, where is your proof of ownership?"

The Minister of Compassion then interrupted Dr. Williams to inform him Simone was not on trial, and that ownership of the formula could eventually be sorted out.

"Dr. Williams, it seems that your intentions were rather transparent earlier in the proceedings. I am certain that with the aid of legal experts here in Switzerland we will be able to find a solution to this question of ownership. Just as the Minister was finishing up addressing Dr. Williams' issue of claim to the formula there was some unexpected activity in the rear of the chamber.

The assistant to the Speaker entered the Chamber and spoke directly to him. The Minister became aware of this activity and smiled at Simone.

"As Speaker of the Chamber, I realize that the proceeding has stretched our normal process and protocol. If the members of the WCN would indulge, I would like to introduce an invited guest to the proceedings."

The Speaker nodded to Kiko who then spoke.

"If the members of the Council would permit, may I introduce to you a Mr. Samuel Bonade."

Simone's eyes widened as Samuel began to walk over to where the Minister was standing. Kiko, who had entered the center of the Chamber, shook his hand and welcomed him to the proceedings, then informed the members that the unexpected guest wanted to say a few words.

Dr. Williams began to verbally object to this break in protocol, but the members began applauding, drowning his objections out. Samuel stepped onto the platform to speak.

"Good evening. My name is Samuel and I am Simone's, I mean Madame Oppenheimer's brother. I have traveled with my sister Lucy who is standing there in the back of the room. My sister and I are honored to be here."

Samuel then waved at Lucy and looked over at Simone. I couldn't believe the expression on Simone's face. It was a combination of both joy and surprise. As Samuel continued speaking Simone moved closer to him.

"Hello Simone. I am so proud of you and so is the Doctor, I know. We are here because sometimes people that are just trying to do good need some help, and after all, that is what family is for. To think back on the time that you and the Doctor were in the kitchen with this water stuff and I had no clue. Well, it seems to have all worked out, just fine." Simone wiped a tear from her eye and Kiko walked over to put his hand on her shoulder for support.

Samuel needed no further encouragement than seeing the expression on Simone's face to continue.

"I know that there was something you were looking for just before leaving St. John. Believe it or not our sister Lucy took it for safekeeping. Well, sort of."

Simone began to smile and nodded that she knew what Samuel meant.

"I believe she realizes now that you had been trying to do something good. Isn't that so Lucy?"

Lucy enthusiastically nodded from the back of the room in the same manner she did in church answering to a hallelujah. I'm glad she understands that.

I am also glad that those two guys standing in front of you here listened to me too."

Simone now stepped over to where Samuel was standing and took his hand. He turned to her and said loud enough for those in the chamber to hear.

"I heard that there is a question as to who owns the formula. Well, me and Lucy are here to give you the answer."

Samuel looked out into the room and encouraged Simone to do the same. It was at that moment she noticed a young woman standing in front of Lucy. It was Isabel. In her hands was the recipe box. She smiled as she walked towards Simone.

Simone reached with both hands to take the recipe box and handed it over to Kiko then knelt and embraced her daughter. Without hesitation Kiko opened the box to discover the registered patent for the formula. The documentation indicated that ownership of the patent for the formula belonged to Isabel Simone Oppenheimer.

Epilogue

It was true what Samuel had told us, 'Your past is your future and your future is part of your past'. What you do in life becomes part of your history and that affects what happens to you in the future. We understood that better than ever as we boarded our flight back to NY. After a few more days in Geneva to celebrate reunions, new connections and accomplishments, it was time to say goodbye.

Kiko spent the last evening with us in Geneva chatting about the brilliance that was demonstrated the night we were all at the WCN. He was so very proud of Simone for her dedication and passion to see the Doctor's idea come to fruition. Most of all he loved the adventure that we all became a part of and told us that our "code orange" diplomatic status was in place for life. He promised to visit us in NY and told us he could get tickets to see the musical Hamilton anytime we liked. He told us he knew people.

We learned shortly after our return that Dr. Wu was rewarded by his government for his efforts. His reward was the freedom to choose to live anywhere he wanted. His choice was to return to Shanghai and continue working in the laboratory at the museum free of government surveillance. To his delight his terms were met and he continued to find an expedient way to replace the faulty purification system left behind by Blue Water International. He promised to keep in touch with Simone and visit us in NY during the holidays telling us it was his favorite time of the year and how much he missed the Christmas show at Radio City, mostly seeing the Rockettes perform.

As for Dr. Williams, he had been reassigned to a small community college in Texas to research the pros and cons of fracking. We were assured that we wouldn't see him anytime too soon in NYC.

Simone, Samuel, and Lucy returned to St. John with Isabel. They agreed that it would be best that Isabel ease into her connection with her past to ensure a happy future. Lucy insisted she hold on to Simone's recipe box for a while to try out some of the French recipes that had been collected. Samuel told Simone that he was going to put some work into the beach house so that she and Isabel could live comfortably and he was going to find his own place, not too far from them and not too close to Lucy. Simone said she and Isabel needed to spend time catching up and thinking about their future, mostly Isabel's education.

John and I went back to our routine in New York, which included planning our next trip. We were back for only a month when we got a call from Simone. She started out telling us how wonderful things were going with Isabel. They were making up for a lot of lost time and doing a lot of retail damage along the way. Towards the end of the call she asked what we thought about being Godfathers to Isabel. They were thinking of sending her to New York for college after she finished up with her studies on St Thomas, which was only a few years away. We told her we would immediately start preparing her room.

THE END

Made in the USA
Coppell, TX
11 January 2020

14389752R00154